"I'm not sure getting muc

Marc released her. "What do you accomplish?"

"Finding you a wife so you'll back off foreclosing on my business."

He stepped back, feeling as if he'd been slapped. "I haven't forgotten our agreement, Rennie. You do your part and I'll live up to mine."

Without another word, he turned and left. How dare she complain about their kiss? It was no big deal. He was on a wife hunt and needed Rennie to help. Their relationship was solely business. So why the anger at her comment? Her purpose was to introduce him to a possible mate. In exchange he'd forget the business loan.

It was a sensible arrangement.

So why did her kisses tempt him so much? Why had he considered making an attempt at friendship? Why did he want Rennie so much, when she was totally opposite to his picture of an ideal wife?

Dear Reader,

Get ready to meet the world's most eligible bachelors: they're sexy, successful and, best of all, they're all yours!

This month in Harlequin Romance® we bring you the latest in our great new series BACHELOR TERRITORY. A series of six books with two things in common—they're all predominantly written from the hero's point of view and they're absolutely wonderful!

This month's book is *Wanted: Perfect Wife* by Barbara McMahon. In November look out for Lucy Gordon's heartwarming contribution to BACHELOR TERRITORY, *Be My Girl*!

Happy Reading!

The Editors

Wanted: Perfect Wife

Barbara McMahon

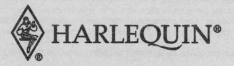

TORONTO • NEW YORK • LONDON
AMSTERDAM • PARIS • SYDNEY • HAMBURG
STOCKHOLM • ATHENS • TOKYO • MILAN • MADRID
PRAGUE • WARSAW • BUDAPEST • AUCKLAND

If you purchased this book without a cover you should be aware that this book is stolen property. It was reported as "unsold and destroyed" to the publisher, and neither the author nor the publisher has received any payment for this "stripped book."

ISBN 0-373-03521-7

WANTED: PERFECT WIFE

First North American Publication 1998.

Copyright © 1998 by Barbara McMahon.

All rights reserved. Except for use in any review, the reproduction or utilization of this work in whole or in part in any form by any electronic, mechanical or other means, now known or hereafter invented, including xerography, photocopying and recording, or in any information storage or retrieval system, is forbidden without the written permission of the publisher, Harlequin Enterprises Limited, 225 Duncan Mill Road, Don Mills, Ontario, Canada M3B 3K9.

All characters in this book have no existence outside the imagination of the author and have no relation whatsoever to anyone bearing the same name or names. They are not even distantly inspired by any individual known or unknown to the author, and all incidents are pure invention.

This edition published by arrangement with Harlequin Books S.A.

® and TM are trademarks of the publisher. Trademarks indicated with ® are registered in the United States Patent and Trademark Office, the Canadian Trade Marks Office and in other countries.

Printed in U.S.A.

CHAPTER ONE

MARC FOSTER stood at the side of the crowded room letting the conversations swirl around him. He took a sip of the champagne—Dom Perignon unless he missed his guess. Only the best for this crowd. He looked across the room where Suzanne Barclay held court. She purported to be his date for the evening, not that she'd spent much time with him, or anyone else for that matter. Suzanne liked to flit and flirt and show off before as many people as possible.

He studied her dispassionately from across the room. Her sleek blond hair was cut short in a sophisticated style that emphasized her high cheekbones and her almond-shaped cat's eyes. The slinky black gown she wore highlighted her best features, the curves that declared her all woman. But she laughed rather shrilly, and seemed to constantly be switching empty glasses for full ones.

He adjusted the sleeve of his tuxedo and noted the time.

A stunning woman, and she knew it. But he didn't care. She wasn't what he sought, after all. A shame, really. On the surface, she met all his requirements.

"Marc?"

He looked around and smiled. Keith Hazelwood was a longtime friend. Marc suspected he would be here tonight.

"Keith, good to see you."

"I admit surprise to see you. What are you doing here, Marc? This isn't the kind of event you usually attend."

"I'm escorting Suzanne Barclay," Marc murmured.

At Keith's grimace, Marc lifted an eyebrow. "Something wrong?"

Keith shook his head. "Suzanne isn't exactly on my top-ten list, that's all." He glanced across the room to the tall blonde, his expression one of blatant disapproval.

"Ah, and what list does she make?" Marc asked.

"Last person I'd wanted to be stranded on a desert island with," Keith replied without hesitation. "I didn't know you knew her."

"A recent introduction."

"Mmm."

"Are these charity events always so crowded?" Marc asked as he faced the room again, taking in the diamonds and sapphires that glittered, the designer gowns that offered splashes of vibrant color contrasting so sharply with the black tuxedos. The ballroom at the St. Francis Hotel seemed to overflow. Standing well over six feet gave him an advantage when studying the crowd. Marc was used to taking advantage whatever the circumstances.

"If you'd come to some of them, you'd know that they are. Everyone likes to be seen at these things. It's considered an event, and once here you are supposed to try to donate more than the next man. But only if you are sure everyone knows exactly the amount on your check," Keith said.

"You're getting cynical in your old age, Keith." Marc scanned the room again, recognizing acquaintances and business associates. He didn't count the majority of people here his friends. In fact, Keith was probably the only true friend he had in the room. The two of them went back a long time.

"If so, I'm only catching up with you. What's the deal, Marc? Why are you here tonight, and with Suzanne Barclay of all people?" Keith asked after a moment. "I've never known you to socialize at an event like this. Is it business?"

Marc shrugged. "Just looking."

"For what?"

Marc hesitated, then spoke slowly. He didn't often share his personal plans or ambitions with anyone. But Keith had known him when he was the kid from the wrong side of the tracks, working two part-time jobs and studying constantly to keep his grades up for his scholarship at Stanford University. Keith had been born with a silver spoon—hell, an entire service—in his mouth. Yet the two of them, oddly enough, had become friends that first day at Stanford.

"Looking for a wife," Marc said, turning to catch his friend's reaction. Keith didn't disappoint him.

"A wife?" Keith stared at him in stunned surprise. "I thought you didn't believe in love and all that stuff."

"You're correct, I don't. What does that have to do with anything?" Marc asked impatiently. "Are you going to tell me there are no women out there who would take me on as a husband because I don't love them?"

"Half the women in the city would take you on, with your money and looks. You know that. But that kind of a relationship would give you the short end of the stick."

"Not if that's all I want."

"And what do you want, exactly?"

"Someone to start a family with, and provide what I don't have now."

"Suzanne Barclay?" Keith scoffed.

"Let's just say she's in the running."

"Forget it, Marc, she's not the one for you."

"No?"

"Not Suzanne. What are you looking for, entrée into the highest of San Francisco's society? Money? Family? Roots?"

"Breeding," Marc said softly, an edge to his voice.

Keith scanned the crowded ballroom, returned his gaze to his friend. "Look, I know where you're coming from, with your background and all. But I think you're plumb crazy. You don't marry some woman just for breeding."

"You do if you want to make sure your kids never have the problems I had as a child."

"Get real, Marc, with your millions, no kid of yours is ever going to come close to the problems you had."

"I want more than what money can buy. I want him to have the right family, the right connections, go to the right schools." Not have to claw and scratch his way to the top like his father, he thought. His son would start out with everything in his favor. And Marc meant to see his son had all the advantages—including a father while he was growing up. He wasn't getting any younger. Time to find a wife and start his family.

"Suzanne drinks. Her mother's a lush and her father's on the verge of bankruptcy. They give a good show, but they are not in the top echelons of society. You've been in that ivory business tower of yours too long if you think they are. Time to mingle and get to know these people before doing something so entangling as marriage. If the marriage didn't take, you'll be stuck with a ton of alimony."

"I don't plan to enter into marriage thinking it's going to end," Marc said calmly.

"Then you better be damn sure you get what you want first time."

"I agree."

Keith ran his fingers through his hair in frustration. "Marc, you aren't going to rush into this, are you?"

"I'll be thirty-six on my next birthday, I hardly think I'm rushing into anything. I could be close to forty by the time a baby arrives. I'd like to be young enough to enjoy him."

"You can't just run after some woman and marry her."

"I'm not just running after some woman, I'm very particular in what I want."

"You may be some hot-shot financial whiz, but when it comes to knowing what's what in San Francisco society, you're a babe in the woods. You haven't made enough contacts to know who's worth cultivating and whom you should avoid. Business is one thing, this is different," Keith protested.

"I'm sure I can manage," Marc said stiffly.

"What you need is someone who can let you know about these people," Keith said impulsively. "Someone who knows the backgrounds, the skeletons in the closets and isn't afraid to share that information."

Marc gave his friend a sardonic smile, and shook his head. "Planning to vet my choices?" he asked.

"I don't know, maybe. You don't know these people like I do. You don't know who's in financial difficulty, and who is just not quite top drawer. I've been around them all my life. I know the inside gossip."

"A lot of which I can find out. Just like I discover which stocks have the best prospective, which bonds are the most lucrative, which start-up ventures hold the most promise."

"Marc, darling." The tall, sleek woman they'd been discussing drifted over to him and slid her arm possessively into the crook of his. Pouting artfully, she batted her eyes at Keith before gazing adoringly up at Marc. "I've had enough of this party, darling. Why don't we go and have one of our own?"

"If you are tired of being here, we can leave," he said politely. But there would be no private party. He'd had enough and Keith was right. Suzanne wasn't the woman he wanted to be the mother of his son.

"Good to see you again, Keith. Call and set up lunch sometime," Marc said, covering Suzanne's hand with his own. He noticed the glances people threw his way, the speculation that ran rampant. When Suzanne preened a bit, he knew she'd seen it, as well, and apparently jumped to the same conclusion as the others. But he hadn't come this far to be caught in any snare not of his own choosing.

"Monday," Keith said. "I'll be by your office late Monday morning and we'll go to lunch then."

Marc escorted the lovely Suzanne home. She was not pleased at the abrupt ending to their evening, but Marc didn't really care. His time was too valuable to waste with someone unsuitable.

"Good night, Suzanne." He prepared to leave her at her door.

"Call me, Marc," she said, her eyes glittering in suppressed frustration.

He smiled, but didn't commit.

"Mr. Hazelwood is here." Rachel's efficient voice announced Keith's arrival over the intercom Monday at noon. Marc wished on Sunday that he hadn't told Keith his plans. He didn't want a lecture during lunch, or to listen to any of Keith's schemes to choose the right wife. Keith was one of the few people in the world who could not be intimidated by Marc. Sometimes there was a downside to long-term friends.

Besides, he'd made up his mind. Examining all the aspects of marriage, he'd determined that choosing a suitable bride from one of the top families in San Francisco would insure the best for any children, and wouldn't hurt current business ventures. Marc was pragmatic and goal oriented. He knew his money and success in the market would be a strong complement to the breeding and background of his future wife. A perfect blending of assets to form a strong bond.

"Send him in." Marc remained another moment by the large window, gazing over the other high-rise office buildings comprising San Francisco's financial district. Hearing the click at the door, he moved from the window and crossed the room as Keith entered.

They gripped hands in greeting.

"I've got it," Keith said.

"What?" Marc asked, shrugging into his suit jacket. "Not the flu, I hope?"

"No, the solution to your problem. To both our problems, as a matter of fact."

"I didn't know we both had a problem," Marc said as they left for lunch. They walked down the street to the small bar and grill on the corner of Montgomery. The restaurant was crowded, but the hostess knew Marc by sight and reputation and quickly found a secluded table.

Once their orders had been given, Keith sat back, raised his water glass in a mock toast and nodded. "I've got the solution to your problem. And in exchange, you can help me out with mine."

Marc raised an eyebrow. "Indeed. And is that a goal of mine, helping you out?"

Keith shook his head, laughing softly. "Probably not, but it will do you good once in a while to help out a friend."

"Especially when I have so few of them."

"You'd have more than you needed if you'd let anyone close to you," Keith fired back bluntly.

"My life is going just how I want it," Marc replied.

Knowing when to back off, Keith nodded, then continued, "Right. That's why you want to get married."

"Haven't you thought about it?" Marc asked. Keith was the same age. Didn't he also long for a family, for a new generation to leave behind when his time was up?

"Of course. When Betsy was alive, I thought we'd marry and have a slough full of kids. I haven't met anyone I've loved as much since she died."

Marc said nothing. He remembered how his friend had loved Betsy Springer. Her death had hit him hard.

"But we're not talking about me, my friend, we're talking about you and your scheme to marry into some highfalutin society family who can trace its roots back to the *Mayflower*."

"The gold rush would do," Marc murmured, resigned to hearing Keith out.

"I have a plan," Keith said, ignoring Marc's comment.

"You have the perfect solution to finding the right woman?" Marc asked skeptically.

"Rennie," Keith said proudly.

"Rennie?" Marc asked. Was the word supposed to mean something to him?

"My cousin Rennie. She can introduce you to the

right people, give you some background on the women themselves, match you up with the perfect mate.''

"You expect your cousin to play matchmaker?'' Marc asked slowly, his eyes narrowing as he studied Keith across the table. He didn't even know the woman.

"Sort of.''

"Sort of.'' Marc continued to stare at his friend. "How does this help you?''

Keith smoothed his tie, an obvious nervous gesture. "Hear me out, Marc. I figure this could go both ways, she'll help you and you can help her. And helping her in this case would help me.'' Keith cleared his throat.

Marc narrowed his eyes. "Spill it all, Keith.''

"Rennie is in a bit of a bind. And you're the cause.''

"I don't even know a Rennie.''

"No, but Brad Peterson does.''

"Ah, I begin to get the picture.'' Marc nodded, his expression forbidding. "Let me guess. This Rennie persuaded Brad to invest in some wild business scheme, and now she can't pay the return.''

"Something like that, only her business isn't so wild. I think she needs a bit of help getting the place off the ground. But since Brad left—''

"Was fired, you mean? He had no sense of business. We'd be flat busted if he'd continued,'' Marc interjected in a hard tone.

"Be that as it may, your company underwrote my cousin's new business. Now that Brad is gone, your new guy is pressing to call the loan. She can't make it. I don't want her to go under. Cut her some slack, give her a bit of time, that's all I'm asking. I think she can pull it off. I wouldn't ask if I didn't think so, you know that, Marc.''

Marc studied his friend for a long moment. "And in exchange for this bit of time, she'll find me a wife?"

Keith winced. "Well, let's just say we can get her to introduce you to possible mates. Rennie can't really force anyone to go out with you, or marry you. But she can introduce you to the kind of woman you are looking for—not someone like Suzanne Barclay."

"How much does this Rennie owe me?"

"A lot."

"You're worth a lot," Marc murmured.

"Rennie needs help, but she's too damn stubborn and proud to accept it from the family. I thought this would make it a business deal—for both of you."

"Business deal? This isn't my idea of business, Keith."

"I don't know, Marc. The way you're going about looking for a wife isn't very romantic. In fact it smacks of business to me. Just think about it, Marc. That's all I'm asking. Rennie has a small shop, a bridal salon. She started it a couple of years ago and is barely making ends meet, yet I think she does good work, always seems busy. I think she needs someone to help on the business side. It's not as if you're going to lose anything by delaying on forcing her out. Give her a chance, and see if you can spot where she needs to tighten up or do something to turn the place around. It gives you a better shot at recapturing your capital, and with Rennie's help, you could end up with the best trophy bride San Francisco has to offer."

"Keith, I do not run shops," Marc said distinctly.

"Of course not, who would expect you to? Marc, it's a bridal shop, not something a man would be involved in. But you could look over her books, make sure she's doing things correctly. And then advise her where the business is weak and how to shore it up. That kind of thing. An afternoon's work at most.''

''Do you know what I charge for that kind of service?'' Marc said ominously.

Keith grinned. ''A bundle. Rennie couldn't afford a minute of your time if she had to pay you for it. But that's the beauty of my plan, she gives you something money can't even buy, introductions to all the right people, and inside information on the prospective brides you couldn't get elsewhere.''

Marc shook his head. ''I think you're crazy.''

''Give it some thought. I'll run it by Rennie and the two of you can take it from there,'' Keith said enthusiastically.

''And who exactly is Rennie?'' Marc asked. He would give it some thought, like four seconds, then tell Keith to keep his damn-fool ideas to himself in the future. Marc didn't need any help finding his own wife.

''Rennie is my cousin. Her mother is Mom's younger sister. When she was a girl, Rennie's mom ran off with a cop. They were in love.''

Marc took a sip of the white wine the waitress had delivered. He was growing just a bit impatient with all Keith's love stories. Never having experienced that emotion, Marc didn't give much credence to it. A purely business arrangement seemed much more likely to succeed over the long haul.

''So they got married and lived happily ever after,'' Marc muttered dryly.

Keith nodded. ''Until Uncle Will died. Killed by some druggie. He left them nothing. It was just the two of them, practically destitute.''

''Didn't your aunt move back home?''

Keith shook his head. ''Nope, too proud. And too

stubborn—same trend you'll find in Rennie. They stuck it out on their own, poor as church mice, from the way my mother tells it.''

"So you want help for your poor-as-a-church-mouse cousin—"

"Hey, I'm not finished. Hold on and hear the rest. The part that makes Rennie the perfect solution for this problem.''

Marc glanced impatiently at his watch. Where was lunch? The service didn't usually take this long. He'd made a mistake in telling Keith about his search for a bride. Now he had to get through lunch and send the man on his way. Once back in the office, he'd have Fielding check into the loan agreement for this Rennie's business.

"When Rennie was ten, Aunt Susan married Theo Quackenbush.''

"Talk about old money and old family,'' Marc murmured, his interest picking up.

"Right. Theo sent Rennie to the best schools. She's friends with all the blue bloods of San Francisco. She's known most of these women for years, from before most of them were teenagers. And she knows the gossip surrounding each.'' Keith sat back, a look of supreme satisfaction on his face.

"And you think Rennie will gladly jump in to help me find a wife from this illustrious pool?'' Marc asked, knowing that was exactly what his friend had thought.

"I think so,'' Keith hedged.

"Ah,'' Marc said. "There's something more.''

The waitress placed their platters before them. Marc took a moment to savor the pleasing look of the still-sizzling steak. A far cry from what the poor boy from the Tenderloin used to eat. Those days were gone forever—he didn't even like thinking about them. But he never forgot them. He had worked hard to insure he never returned. And he was determined no child of his would ever experience what he'd lived through.

A quick glance around the restaurant assured him he had succeeded. The men surrounding him were successful businessmen, bankers, financiers, stockbrokers, corporate executives—the movers and shakers of San Francisco. He'd joined their ranks through sheer determination and hard work.

He glanced at Keith. "Let me think about it," he temporized. Normally he'd give his friend a flat go to hell. But something made him want to ease his refusal. Maybe it was because years ago Keith had stood by his friend, the rich boy from Woodside and the poor kid from the Tenderloin.

"I'll call Rennie after lunch. I'll give her your number. The two of you can work things out, okay?" Keith asked.

"Sure." When Rennie called, Marc would simply mention he had decided to forgo her services. She couldn't be too interested in setting up a girlfriend with a blind date, especially with a man she didn't know.

"Besides your love life, how are things going?" Keith asked, changing the subject. Soon the two men began to discuss business strategies and successes.

Night had fallen by the time Marc leaned back in his chair and looked out the big windows that lined one wall of his office. The City by the Bay sparkled. The lights outlining the Bay Bridge seemed to shimmer across the inky water. The TransAmerica pyramid gleamed in the darkness, lights shining from offices where men and women worked late. He stood and wandered to the window for a closer look. He loved the city. Born and raised here, he never wanted to live anywhere else.

When his phone rang, he wondered who would call his private line at—he glanced at his watch as he crossed the room—eight thirty-five.

"Foster."

"Hello, is this Marc Foster?" a breathless feminine voice inquired.

"Speaking."

"Well you are hard to track down. I tried calling you at home several times since six, but there was never an answer. I thought you'd be home by six, even with the rush-hour traffic. Now I know why your phone there just rang and rang. Do you always work so late?"

"Who is this?" His habits were no one's business but his own.

"Oh, sorry, I guess I jumped ahead. This is Rennie Morgan. I'm Keith Hazelwood's cousin. He said you were expecting my call. I tried to call this afternoon, well actually, I wanted to call then, but things kept coming up. And this isn't the kind of thing you want to discuss with a shop full of brides. So I waited until I thought you'd be home. I've been trying all evening. Finally I wondered if you were still at work and you are. So that's good. I mean that I found you, not that it's good to be working so late."

Marc wondered when she was going to let up enough so he could get a word in edgewise.

"I wanted to reach you today if I could so we could get this all cleared up. Keith is my favorite cousin, but he does get carried away sometimes. And some of his schemes are quite outlandish, like this one. I expect you must know that since he said you've been friends from Stanford days. I can't think why we haven't met at some point over the years, but there you are, we haven't. You must not attend his parties. Which shows some sense on your part, they can get pretty wild. Which isn't much like Keith these days, is it? I mean he's become so conservative and all. Probably taking his responsibilities at work seriously. Which will please Uncle Keith.''

''Miss Morgan—''

''Call me Rennie. The thing is, Mr. Foster, I don't run a dating service. Keith said you wanted me to introduce you to some of my friends with an end objective of marriage. I think marriage is a great end objective. One I may have myself some day. But I don't run a dating service. I do weddings. That's usually long after the first date.''

''Keith said you ran a bridal salon,'' Marc said.

''Yes, I do. Brides and Bows. Actually bows is spelled b-o-w-s, but I'm hoping people will think of it as a play on words, *beaux,* like boyfriends, you know? Actually, you should know all about it, your firm gave me the start-up money. Which is why I thought it rather mean to then threaten to yank it away. I don't have the money to repay the initial loan yet, but I'm working on it and one day I'll be able to repay you everything. The thing is your Mr. Fielding doesn't seem inclined to take that view. He is trying to force me into liquidation. That would end the business, which seems dumb because then you'd never get all your money back.''

''Keith indicated you could use some financial advice.''

She was silent for a moment. ''Actually, that's Keith's idea, and probably Aunt Patty's. I'm doing fine if you'd just call off Mr. Fielding. And let's face facts, Mr. Foster, there's no way Marc Foster of Foster Associates, one of this city's largest and most successful financial services house, is going to bail out a small bridal salon. I'm squeaking out a profit, and I like what I do, but it's not big business. Not like yours is. You can spare the money a little longer."

For some reason her assumption that he wouldn't work with a small firm rankled. He'd started out small himself. One reason he started his venture capital branch was to help others along the way, as well as turn a tidy profit. Marc had been fully prepared to refuse her help, but now because she wasn't offering, perversely he wanted it.

"So you won't help me?" he asked softly.

"I think one of San Francisco's most eligible bachelors won't have any trouble attracting women. I've seen your picture in the paper, you know. You're—"

The abrupt silence went on for several seconds until Marc prompted, "I'm what?"

"Well, let's just say a hunk and let it go at that."

Something touched his sense of humor and he laughed softly. He'd never heard that term referred to himself. "Maybe you should tell me more."

"I think that would be pointless. I'm glad we had this chat. Don't let Keith railroad you into doing things you don't want."

"I assure you, Ms. Morgan, I never do anything I don't want." Not anymore.

"Call me Rennie. And I'm glad you are in the position to do just what you want. Sorry to call you at work, but if you keep such long hours you have to expect people will call you there for personal things. Why aren't you home?"

"I beg your pardon?"

"Not my business, I know. But it's getting late. I bet you've not even had dinner. You should keep better hours," she scolded gently. "I know I would work all night sometimes I get so caught up in a design, but I discipline myself to quit and do something frivolous. It restores creative juices, don't you know. And I would think you could use some of that, as well."

"Creative juices?" Intrigued by this fireball on the phone, Marc leaned back in his chair and crossed his legs, placing his feet on the edge of the desk. "I assure you I eat fine, Rennie. But maybe having a wife would insure I kept better hours. Are you sure you won't help in finding me one?" he said smoothly, waiting to hear what she'd say next.

"The problem as I see it, Mr. Foster, besides the fact that I don't run a dating service, is I know nothing about you. Well, that's not strictly true, because I read the newspapers. But I don't know about your family, your background, what you like to do for fun, what your plans are for the future. How could I match you up with someone if I don't know you? You see the problem? And I do have to work at the shop. If your firm is making threats to foreclose on my note, I have to do something to keep going."

"I see."

"Keith is so impulsive. These are my friends we're talking about. I want to make sure they get a good deal, too."

"An introduction is all I believe Keith suggested, not delivering them ready for the altar," Marc interjected.

"Oh. Well, yes, of course. But even so...I really can't do it."

"I'd be happy to look over your records, perhaps hold off on calling the loan," he said slowly. At least until he met her. He couldn't remember being so intrigued in years. He found himself curious to meet her in person.

"You're serious, aren't you? You really want me to help you find a bride?"

"No, I want you to introduce me to some eligible women. There's a difference. I can take it from the introduction."

She remained silent a long time.

"What are you looking for?" she asked at last.

"I want someone from a good family with a good pedigree, who knows how to move in society and would be an asset to me in business." Someone to give him the background he lacked himself. To provide an extended family for his son.

"Sounds like you're looking for a dog or something. Most people come without a pedigree," she muttered.

"Not a dog. A sleek, sophisticated woman who comes from an excellent family."

"You can fall in love to order?" she asked dubiously.

"I don't expect to fall in love. I am sure over time I will acquire a certain degree of affection for the woman."

"Oh, God, now you do sound like you're getting a dog. A degree of affection? What is a degree? Sounds cold-blooded to me. I think you need to do this on your own. I'll tell Keith we talked and decided to let things go the way they were."

"Foreclosure and all?" he asked sharply.

She hesitated. "So that's the way you want it? I cooperate or you yank my business?"

"I believe it's you who has not managed to make the loan payments. I would merely be exercising my rights under the terms of the agreement." Marc wondered if she cared enough about her business to agree to his terms. He was used to making deals in his favor and he saw nothing to change his methods now.

"I don't know. Wouldn't you consider giving me more time because of your friendship with Keith?"

"No."

"Oh." The silence stretched out endlessly.

"On the other hand, in exchange for your assistance, I would certainly hold off for a reasonable time. Enough probably to let you recoup and repay the loan," Marc said, surprising himself. If the woman didn't want to help, why push the issue? He'd leave the business end to his employees and go on the way he'd started. This had been Keith's idea, not his.

But he found himself intrigued with Rennie Morgan, He wanted to meet her. Did she talk as much in person as on the phone? What did she look like? Nothing like his image of a wife, he was certain. No one who talked this fast and this much could be sleek and sophisticated. Maybe she didn't really know anyone who would measure up to his ideal wife. He had only Keith's word that she knew everyone.

"You're looking for a trophy bride, aren't you? Someone to show off and deck in the family jewels and have other men envy you." Her tone was sharp.

"Family jewels?" he murmured.

"Everyone has them, gaudy things that some previous generation bought, just to flaunt their wealth. You don't mention kids, is that part of the deal? Do you want any?"

"Yes, I want a son." The entire purpose of the exercise was to acquire a son to leave his business and fortune to. He planned to be a better father to his child than he'd ever received. And he wanted his son to have the best mother money could buy.

"To leave everything to, I'm sure. No daughters?" There was an edge in her voice.

He paused for a moment, surprised at the thought. "Yes, I would like a daughter or two," he said slowly. The idea sounded appealing, though he hadn't a clue how to raise a daughter. But his wife would know. She'd be an expert at all that.

"Good, I like little girls better than little boys. Must be from hanging around Keith when we were little. He could really be a pain. I think you can attract just the kind of woman you want without any help from me. Go get your picture in the paper again and then start trolling at the parties that abound in the city."

"I'm not sure that will work," he murmured, knowing she sounded ready to end the conversation. He wanted to extend the call.

"Why not?"

"I took Suzanne Barclay to the—"

"Suzanne? No wonder Keith said you needed help. Suzanne has a drinking problem. Her mother is a drunk and her father gambles all the time. The family had pots of money at one time, but now I hear they are seeking to replenish the family coffers by latching onto some rich young man. Did you ask her out?"

"Yes, I did." For a moment, he resented the position Suzanne had placed him in, then shook his head. When he started in the investment arena, he'd had a great deal to learn. Having mastered that, he almost forgot there were other areas in which he was not so knowledgeable. And the ways of San Francisco society were one of them. Maybe Keith was right, he could use a bit of an insight on the women he considered for a mate.

"So Suzanne is someone I should stay clear of?"

"If you value your sanity, I would. Besides, if you're looking for someone to help your business, you don't want to be tied to a gambler and a lush."

"I can see your services would be invaluable. I appear to have a lot to learn about this. Will you meet me tomorrow to discuss this further?"

"Your poor-little-me tactics won't work, Marc Foster. I know how ruthless you can be. You don't need me or anyone else to get you what you want. This is it for me. I'm really not interested. Do your damnedest about my shop, I'll fight it. Goodbye."

"Goodbye, Rennie," Marc said to a dial tone. Slowly he set the receiver down. Another first—he couldn't remember anyone hanging up on him before. Slowly he looked out the window at the sparkling lights in the other buildings. Rennie Morgan could be forgiven if she thought she'd had the last word. They hadn't met yet, and she didn't know him. But that would change tomorrow. He'd meet her and talk her into helping him. Something told him she was more emotionally involved with her business than most people. Probably *loved* it.

Keith had been correct, he did need someone who knew her way around society. Rennie might be just the person to help. And if he decided she was the one, he would insure she helped, or lose her business. It would be interesting to see how she handled that.

He reached for the phone, dialed a familiar number. "Keith? It's Marc. I have a few questions about your cousin Rennie."

CHAPTER TWO

MARC pulled his Mercedes into the tight space parking spot on Union Street. The trendy San Francisco neighborhood had more shops and boutiques per block than any other part of the city. From antique stores to bakeries to fashionable salons, Union Street catered to the elite and monied of San Francisco.

He walked back a block to the discrete gold and white sign: Brides and Bows. He hesitated, unlike him. Usually once he made up his mind he charged ahead, knowing he had weighed all the information before making a decision. Last night, he had decided to drop by and meet Rennie in person. To further discuss the odd deal Keith had proposed.

It was past the lunch hour, she should be hard at work, where he hoped to catch her unaware in order to learn a bit more about the intriguing woman. He knew he held the high cards in this deal, if she didn't cooperate, he'd call the loan and close her business. If it looked like it had potential, he'd put another manager in and see if he could recoup his investment that way.

He pushed open the door, frowning at the tingling bell that sounded. The inside was frilly, lacy and feminine. Gilded French Provincial chairs and a brocade-covered Queen Anne settee formed a small waiting area to the left. A lacy bridal dress was displayed by a mannequin with a sweet young face. Accessories were artistically draped on tables, display cabinets and on the one long counter at the right side of the showroom.

Marc looked around, feeling decidedly uncomfortable. He felt at home in a boardroom, or at a football game—not amid trappings of fairy-tale love and romance. Tall and muscular, his body was not built for the dainty furniture that welcomed customers. Never one for lace and satin, for a moment he felt totally out of his element. He had never lived with a woman, nor become more involved than an occasional night in a woman's bed. He knew nothing about bridal wares. He believed he could go his entire life without knowing.

"Hello, may I help you?"

A tall blonde entered from the doorway in the rear of the store. Elegantly attired in a stylish red suit, her hair worn up in a sophisticated French braid, she looked exactly like what he had in mind for his wife. Had Keith set him up? He knew Marc wanted someone sleek and sophisticated. Was this Rennie? Had the lure of the foreclosure been Keith's way to force a meeting? Was that why he insisted Marc use his cousin to find a wife?

"Rennie?" he asked as his eyes skimmed over the discrete curves, the long, slender legs encased in silk stockings.

The blonde smiled. "No, she's in the back working on a dress. I'll get her for you."

Marc nodded, curiously relieved. He studied the boutique while he waited. He didn't know much about weddings, though he figured he'd find out more than he wanted when he married. This boutique appeared to have everything a woman could possibly dream up. He looked at frilly little pillows, wondering what they were used for.

"Oh, my God, Marc Foster in the flesh. Come to inspect the merchandise? See what it could get on the block?"

At the sound of the surprised voice, he turned, and stared right into a pair of dancing blue eyes.

He'd never seen merry eyes before, he thought. Slowly he took in the gamine grin, one side a trifle higher than the other. Skin that looked like a soft blushing rose and a wild mop of curly blond hair completed the picture before him.

She grinned at him as if in genuine delight. "You're even better looking in person. Something about black and white takes away from the reality, don't you think." She came out into the showroom and offered her hand, "I'm Rennie, as I guess you've figured out. You must be serious about this. I did consider that Keith set me up, but I don't think you're the type to play practical jokes, or at least not carry it this far."

"So you're Rennie Morgan." He took her hand. Her grip was firm, and her skin startling warm and soft. He wanted to hold on to her, to trace that softness with his fingers and see if she felt that soft everywhere. He released her and took a step back, surveying the room to cover his momentary loss of concentration. "Nice place."

"If you're into this kind of thing, which I suspect you are not."

He looked back at her, studying her from those wild curls down the tailored silk shirt, the woolen pants to— bare feet!

She followed his gaze and grinned. "I hate shoes. If you were a customer, I'd put them on. That's why I peeped out of the back room first. I always put them on for business. But I really don't like wearing them. Except in winter. Even then I usually wear socks and nothing else unless I go out. Then of course I have to wear something to keep from freezing, or looking like some poor street person.''

Marc met her eyes, trying to ignore the image that popped into his mind of Rennie in nothing but wild curls and socks. Awareness shimmered through him and he felt a tightening of desire low down.

''I came to continue our conversation of last night,'' he said smoothly, refusing to dwell on the tantalizing image that danced in his mind.

''Well, I guess we'll have to since you've gone to all the trouble of coming way over here from Montgomery Street during the height of the day. And I'm grateful you didn't send Mr. Fielding, he is getting to be a bit of a drag. But I don't think we have much to say. What part of no don't you understand?''

''The part that applies to me,'' he said arrogantly. ''Either I get the help I need, or this business becomes mine, lock, stock, and barrel. I'll have a new manager in by tomorrow noon.'' He hadn't made it as far as he had by being easy.

She stared up at him, the light in her eyes dimmed. For a moment Marc wondered if she'd not suspected he'd go that far. He didn't have a philanthropic bent regarding business, it was cut and dried. He did whatever he needed to get ahead. But for a moment, he hesitated. And then frowned, disliking the sensation. He who hesitated lost.

So she was pretty. He'd seen beautiful women before, even dated a few. It didn't matter that she was Keith's cousin. This was business pure and simple. She had something he had decided he wanted. And he'd do what it took to get it.

''Well, that's pretty clear.'' Rennie put her hands on her hips and stared out of the glass window fronting the street—silent for several long minutes. Used to silence in negotiating situations, Marc remained quiet. He'd had years to perfect his skills, he suspected this woman hadn't a clue.

She swung around and glared at him. For an instant he felt a surge of anticipation. So she wasn't going to meekly roll over and play dead?

"First thing I need to do is have my attorney look over the agreement. Probably should have done it when Fielding started nosing around. There's bound to be something I can do to stop you from forcing me to give up my business."

"The contracts we offer are iron-clad. Set up by some of the best attorneys in the city."

"My cousin Clare is pretty good, too," she murmured.

"Another cousin?"

Her eyes narrowed and she stepped closer, tilting back her head to maintain eye contact. Marc refrained from giving in to the instinct to stand even taller just to see her reaction. Amusement lurked, she still intrigued him.

"A good attorney," she said.

"So it's war?"

"If that's your call."

"No, my call is having you introduce me to some eligible single women."

"And if I don't, you take my business. *Try* to take my business."

"Take this business!" His voice brooked no denial. "The choice is yours."

"So let me clarify this. If I introduce you to as many women as I know that fit your requirements for a trophy wife, you'll leave my shop alone?" She met his gaze, her eyes narrowed.

"At least delay the inevitable," he replied, a sweet flush of triumph sweeping through.

"Wait a minute, no delays. I want some guarantee that I keep the boutique."

"If I get a wife, you get the shop. I'll make it a wedding present."

She frowned. "That's weird, the groom giving a wedding present to someone beside the bride. But I accept. It will help tremendously not to have that heavy debt load."

"Don't count your chickens yet, Rennie. I don't have a bride."

"Let me think…"

She walked over to the large picture window and gazed absently out onto busy Union Street, her arms folded beneath her breasts. Turning, Rennie cocked her head as she studied Marc. He watched her, amused again by the change in her attitude. Hadn't she suspected he'd play hardball? Surely her cousin had told her something about him. He wondered what, exactly, Keith had said.

"I can't guarantee a bride, but I can guarantee to introduce you to everyone I think would meet your requirements, once I know what they are. I need to know more about you if I'm to find a compatible match."

Her frown had him wishing she'd smile again. "Such as?"

"I don't know. I hadn't planned to do it." She tapped her index finger against her chin. "Maybe we could get together later at my place and go over some things. I'm really swamped here today, and besides, I don't think you'd take to the constant interruptions that are a part of my business. Tonight would work. I need time anyway to think about what I need to know. I've never done anything like this before. I'm not sure what's involved."

"Who's your assistant?" he asked, plunging into the midst of her monologue lest she never stop.

"Eve? She's taken, if you're thinking of her as a possibility. She's been married, and quite happily I might add, for over three years." Rennie tapped her finger to her chin again and looked him up and down. Walking around him as if surveying a prizefighter, Marc thought in irritation.

"So you want a trophy wife. Sleek, elegant, sophisticated."

His scowl deepened. "I think that is a bit harsh a judgment—trophy wife. I want the mother of my children to have an impeccable background."

"You could find her yourself."

"It's faster to have someone screen the candidates for me. This is too important to make a mistake and marry the wrong woman."

"Sounds like business. By all means let's be expeditious," she said, wrinkling her nose.

"A bit different from stocks and bonds, but not much. I'm looking for a long-term merger of two people's lives."

"Oh, God, a merger! Right, that tells me something. Now to find someone who thinks like a computer."

"I don't want a business partner, I want a wife."

"Okay, we'll sit down later and discuss all the sterling attributes you want in a wife and I'll see if any of my friends would fit the bill. And since what you really want is a trophy bride, you'll be happy to learn I know a few women who would be content in that role. They like money, like spending it on clothes and jewelry to adorn themselves, don't want to waste energy on emotions like love. They would do you proud."

"Rennie, phone, it's Joanne Pembroke," Eve called from the archway.

"Oh, right. Excuse me, I need to take this call, business you know."

"Take it, I'll wait."

She looked as if she wanted to tell him no, but she turned and hurried back through the doorway. Eve stayed with Marc, smiling slowly. "She's a whirlwind, isn't she? I can't keep up with her, so I no longer try."

"I would have expected her to dress a bit more. . ." He hesitated, not wanting to insult Eve's boss to her employee. But he knew clothes made a difference in business. It had been one of the first things he'd discovered. People are influenced by what other people wear. An expensive suit with all the right accessories gave the impression of confidence, assurance, and wealth. He knew because he'd used that technique when he first started. It had made the difference in more than one business deal.

"You've been with Rennie for two years?" Marc asked.

"Ever since she started the boutique. I was looking for something to fill my days. She more than provided that." Eve smiled again. Marc thought she was probably a major asset to Rennie's boutique.

"Business doing well?" he asked.

Her smile faded. "You have to discuss that with Rennie. That's not my place."

"Probably not doing so or you would have given me a resounding yes." He walked over to one of the wedding dresses. "How much?" he asked.

"That one is twelve hundred dollars."

"For a single dress? Worn one afternoon?" He shook his head in disbelief. That money could be invested and start earning a return, instead of being frittered away for an hour's ceremony. "Why is it on display?" He glanced around. "There aren't any others."

"We made it up for a woman who changed her mind and eloped. We're hoping someone will see it and want to buy it."

"Did she pay for the dress?"

"Only the down payment. We took a loss on it. Rennie is hoping that by displaying it, someone will walk in the door, see it, and fall in love with it."

Love. That was what Rennie dealt in. Marc felt uncomfortable. He didn't believe in the emotion and hoped that wasn't going to prove a stumbling block in working with Rennie. Obviously she was a hopeless romantic, even based her business on the nebulous emotion of love.

"Sorry about that," Rennie said as she hurried back into the showroom. "I've been waiting to talk with her for ages. She's been out of town. Her wedding is only three weeks away. I wondered if she'd get back in time for it. Now, what else do we need to do? I have a ton of work waiting." Rennie smiled at her friend and stopped some distance from Marc.

He wondered why the distance. For a moment he had the urge to walk right up to her, crowd her against that counter and—

She wasn't very tall, the top of her head barely cleared his shoulder. Her lips looked soft and gentle, damp when she licked them. Her eyes were her best feature, and she frankly watched him, a hint of wariness in her gaze. He wanted to see the shining light that had sparkled when he'd first met her.

"I thought I'd go over your books, see where you

stand, to give me a better feeling for what's needed here, or how far behind you truly are.''

She swallowed. "My books," she repeated, looking at Eve as if for help.

Eve smiled and shrugged her shoulders. "Don't look at me. I don't keep the books."

"Yes, well, actually this is not a very good time," Rennie said, obviously stalling.

"And when would be good?" He suspected instantly that her books must be a total disaster. He wasn't an accountant, he was a financial advisor. His clients were multimillion-dollar corporations with up-to-the-minute record-keeping.

"Tonight, maybe. You're coming over, right?"

He nodded. "Eight be all right?"

"Yes." She gave him her address and walked with him to the door. He had never been escorted from any-place, but that was the feeling he got from Rennie. She was kicking him out, nicely, but definitely.

"Dress casually, I will," she said as she opened the door and almost pushed him out.

Marc heard the bell jingle and the door click behind him. He glanced up the street, wondering whether to confront the woman now, or give in to the amusement that simmered. It had been a long time since he'd felt like this. If ever.

His watch read precisely eight o'clock when Marc knocked at the door to Rennie's Chestnut Street apart-ment. The building smelled musty and old while the parking on the street had proved to be an abomination.

When she opened the door, he felt a clutch of feeling as she smiled up at him.

"You're prompt, but then I expected that. Have you

been waiting out in the hall for the exact moment to knock? Most people arrive a few minutes early or late, but I could have set my clock by you.''

''No need to wait, I timed my arrival to the minute.'' She looked at his suit. ''I thought I said casual.''

''I came from work. And since this is business, I thought this appropriate.''

She had changed into a vibrant pink and blue warm-up suit and pulled her hair away from her face in clips. Her feet were bare.

''Your loss. I like comfort myself. Come in and sit. Can I get you something to drink? Or eat? Did you have dinner?''

''You're not my mother, Rennie. I don't want nor need anything. Let's get to the business at hand.'' Marc refused to be sidetracked by her hospitality, or by his own fascination with her toes.

''All men want to do is cut to the chase, never mind the niceties of social living. I don't know why women bother. Yet we seem to generation after generation.''

Marc ignored her as he walked into her living room. It suited her. Large comfortable chairs and a plump sofa were arranged to provide a warm welcome. He sank into one of the chairs and almost smiled. It provided the perfect support for his large frame. He wondered if she'd bought it for male friends. The smile faded as the thought disturbed him. Did Rennie have a lot of male friends? Close enough to drop by from time to time?

''Good grief, we haven't even started and you're frowning already. What's wrong?''

''Nothing. Let's begin. I have an early appointment tomorrow.''

''And so don't want to stay out late. All right.'' She

sat on the sofa, tucked her feet up beneath her and drew a yellow pad and pencil from the coffee table.

"Yellow's good for creativity, did you know that?" she murmured as she wrote his name on the top.

"I didn't. Are we getting creative with my requirements?"

"Nope. I just like yellow. How old are you?"

"What does that have to do with anything?" he asked.

She looked up. "Well, while some people might not mind being a trophy wife of an older man with pots of money, some would. So I have to know how old you are—"

"I'm hardly an older man. I'm thirty-five," he snapped, already feeling exasperated with Rennie and with himself for allowing this to proceed.

"I'm twenty-six myself. Most of the friends I have who are still eligible for the marriage stakes are around my age. Some might not want to date an older man."

"For God's sake, I'm not an older man. Thirty-five is a man's prime."

"Right— and just what I expected a man of thirty-five to say," she muttered, throwing him a look. "What's your favorite color?"

Marc glared at her. "Rennie," he said, clamping down on the anger that began to simmer. "I don't have a favorite color and what the hell would it matter in being introduced to some woman?"

She sighed and looked at him, her expression serious. "Marc, I need to get a feel for who you are and what you like so I can talk about you to friends. I can't do this if you are going to question every question I ask. If you like green, you're probably a genius. More geniuses like the color green than any other color. If blue—"

"Black. If I have to like a color, make it black," he bit out.

"Matches your heart, eh?" She jotted a note on her pad.

"What's your favorite color?" he asked before she finished writing.

"Mine? Pink. Why?"

He held her gaze for a long moment. Then shrugged. "Just curious." He rose and took off his suit jacket, placing it across the arm of the other chair. Loosening his tie, he sat back down, sprawled his long legs out before him, hooked his thumbs beneath his belt and stared at her.

"Relaxed, huh?" She grinned.

He nodded, his gaze direct.

Rennie caught her breath, looking down at her pad as if flustered.

"Something wrong," he asked as something eased inside. Maybe he wasn't the only one to feel this unexpected pull of attraction, of strong awareness. She was a pretty woman, soft and feminine. Being around her made him more conscious of being a man. It wasn't just that he hadn't had a woman in a while, there was more. Something about her claimed his interest.

Yet she met none of the requirements in what he wanted in a wife. There was nothing sleek or elegant about her. She appeared bright, funny and a bit irreverent. He thought of sunshine and flower gardens when around her. Did other men? Again the thought disturbed. Why should he care what other men thought about Rennie? He was using her to gain his own goal—the perfect blue-blood wife, with strong ties to an old San Francisco family. He'd firm his own place in society and provide the best background possible for any children.

She shook her head, her eyes firmly on her pad. "Nothing's wrong. What's your favorite food?"

"Tacos."

"Tacos?" She looked up, startled.

"Something wrong with tacos?"

"No, only I thought you'd like caviar or filet mignon or something ritzy."

"No, I like tacos. What's your favorite?"

"Shrimp, boiled, shelled, cooled and with lots of cocktail sauce."

"I would have pictured you with chocolate," he said.

She flashed that gamine grin he started to expect around her. "I do like chocolate, it would be perfect after the shrimp."

For the next two hours Rennie asked questions, what books did he read, which movies he liked, which ones he didn't. She asked where he'd traveled, and vacationed. What his favorite thing was to do on a lazy Saturday. For every question she asked him, he asked one of her in return.

When she asked him about growing up, he'd turned the subject. Finally she asked him outright about his parents.

"They are both dead," Marc said flatly.

"How awful, I'm so sorry." Her blue eyes held sadness, concern.

"It happened a long time ago," he said shortly. He didn't need her sympathy.

"We can skip that for now. It's who you are today that will entice a woman."

Marc tried to find out what made Rennie tick as the evening wore on. She perplexed him. She didn't fit any mold he knew, and he liked things tidy. He wanted an explanation. According to Keith, she turned her back on the wealth her stepfather offered, and plunged instead into earning her own living. The schooling she had gratefully accepted, but nothing beyond.

Marc was not used to being around women. The few he knew seemed to expect others to wait on them, to provide them with enough money to purchase everything they wanted, and give them the lifestyle they sought— using his money.

It was what he expected of his wife. She would know how to buy the furnishings for his home to impress people. She would be able to dress appropriately for his position in the business community. And maybe he'd purchase those jewels Rennie had spoken about. Only nothing gaudy, something tasteful and expensive—only the best for his wife. There was nothing wrong in a man making sure others knew he had attained financial security by the baubles he bought his wife.

"That's enough for one night," Rennie said, tossing her scribbled notes on the table and stretching.

The top of the running suit came a bit above her waist, exposing a strip of pale skin.

Marc's gaze instantly dropped there and he wondered if that skin felt softer than her hand had been. He would like to explore that stretch of skin and find out. Hell, he'd like to explore a whole lot more than just that small sliver of skin. He'd like to explore Rennie Morgan herself from tousled curls to pink toes.

"Did you bring your financial records home?" he asked. She'd filled the time with questions, but made no mention of the second part of the deal.

Biting her lip, she looked at him, indecision clearly written on her face.

"Actually, I did. But you don't have to look at them tonight. Another time maybe?" she asked brightly. "It is getting late. If I know you, you'll want to be in the office early tomorrow for that appointment. Right?''

"Tonight's fine." He ignored her red herring.

"I thought you had an early appointment in the morning."

He smiled. "Get the books, Rennie."

"You look like a wolf who's ready to pounce."

"Wolves don't pounce, kittens pounce. Wolves stalk, waiting for the right moment to spring on their prey and take them down."

Her eyes widened and she stared at him for a long moment. Sighing long and hard when Marc remained silent, Rennie rose and flounced into the hallway, resentment evident in every step. Returning moments later, she carried a satchel of papers and one binder. Reluctantly, she crossed the room and thrust them out to him.

She almost dragged her feet like a kid, he thought at he looked at the satchel. He should not have been surprised. He knew small businesses often did their record-keeping differently from major corporations, but this handbag of papers was worse than he expected.

"Do you have any clue how you're doing?" he asked in shock.

"Pretty good, I think. Well, maybe not all that well. I have trouble making ends meet sometimes. Other times I have some extra cash. That's why Keith thought you should check these things out. An even cash flow would go a long way in helping to make the business a success, don't you think?"

"Undoubtedly. I'll look at this and get back to you." He rose and donned his jacket. Actually he planned to have his accountant make some sense out of the mess. He wasn't going to waste his time. And once Stuart straightened out the records, he'd have him teach some basic accounting to Rennie Morgan. If she was serious about running a business, she needed better skills than this.

"What are you doing for lunch on Friday?" she asked.

For a moment he wondered if she were asking him out.

"Why?" She was Keith's cousin, a woman who was helping him find a wife. She wouldn't invite him on a date. He wasn't sure she even liked him.

"I think Marcella Randolph would be a good candidate. I've been thinking about her as we talked. I'll invite her to lunch on Friday. You can accidentally happen upon us. Then I'll invite you to join us. You and Marcella can take it from there," she said, her eyes going forlornly to her papers.

"What time Friday and where?"

"Marcella loves that restaurant near Battery and Montgomery. Sabrina's. How about twelve-thirty?"

"You're on. See you then." He picked up the satchel and headed for the door. Rennie followed him. He could smell her perfume, the fragrance familiar. He had it— strawberry. Fresh and wholesome like she was.

He stopped by the door. Rennie stopped beside him and looked up. Without thinking, without giving any analysis, he leaned over and brushed his lips across hers.

She felt as soft as he'd thought she'd be. And six times sweeter.

"Good night." He left quickly, before she could say a word. And for once he felt the honors were his. She'd been stunned, too much so to even think of talking!

But the joke was on him, he thought a few minutes later as he climbed into his car. He could still feel that petal softness, that sweetness about her. Something intrigued him about Rennie Morgan. He'd best remember theirs was a business deal and ignore the rest.

And avoid kissing her in the future.

By ten the next morning, Marc gave up. He tossed his gold pen down and shoved the prospectus away. He'd been trying to concentrate on the new proposal since his early appointment had ended, but his curiosity ran rampant. He couldn't concentrate. He wanted answers on Rennie's situation.

He quickly went down the hall to Stuart's office. The man had papers piled around, in some sort of order, but it looked like mildly controlled chaos to Marc.

"Get anywhere on Brides and Bows?" he asked.

Stuart looked up and grimaced. "This is the biggest mess I've ever seen. Apparently she jots things down on scrap paper, then drops everything into an envelope until it gets too crowded, then she starts up another envelope. Some bills have notes on them that they've been paid, others don't, yet she doesn't carry the balance on the next one so they have to have been paid. She didn't include the checkbook."

"Will you be able to get a financial reading?" Marc asked.

"I can get something. How accurate, I can't guarantee. This woman needs a few basic accounting lessons."

At five Stuart returned the satchel and binder to Marc, totally exasperated. He had done as much as he could, but had pages of notes and questions. Marc thanked him for the effort and glanced at his watch. It was too late to call her at work. What he'd really like to do was take these books over to her house and sit her down and demand she go through everything with him. Answer every one of Stuart's questions. But it would take more than a couple of hours. Maybe she'd have time that weekend.

Not Saturday. He couldn't make Saturday, he had promised the director he'd be in this Saturday for sure. But maybe Sunday. He'd have to check with her. Later, once she was home.

Marc first called at seven. There was no answer.

Impatient with the delay, he slammed down the receiver. "Where is she?"

Acting on a hunch, he called her shop. The phone rang and rang. Not there.

He tried her home again at seven-thirty, then at eight, then nine.

"Hello?"

"Rennie? This is Marc."

"Hi, what's up?"

"Where have you been?"

"Me? Out. What do you want? Why are you calling me at home?"

"We went over your books today. You almost drove my accountant into quitting." He settled back in his chair, waiting to hear what she had to say. He didn't want to admit how much he'd looked forward to hearing her voice again.

"Well, I have been meaning to get everything organized, but I'm so busy with other things I haven't had the time. I'm much more interested in doing dresses and getting just the right accessories than spending hours doing boring bookkeeping. And Eve doesn't do books. Not that she should, it is my business. Um, did he say how things look?"

"It's hard to determine without your current checkbook. You didn't give me that."

"Well of course not. That's my money, I'm not just handing it over to someone because they want to study my records. I need that, I pay bills, pay Eve, I can't just hand that over. I can read you the balance if you have to have it, but I'm not giving it up!"

"We need to see the individual entries, run a reconciliation. If you have any extra cash, we should explore investment opportunities."

"What? Like there would be more than one? Okay, I want to invest any extra money in something that will pay big dividends that I can use next month if I'm short."

"Everybody wants that."

"Well, isn't that what you do? I mean, everything I've heard about you indicates you're some sort of wunderkind about investments. Making millions for companies who call you in to turn their economics around. Have you ever lost a dime?"

"Yes, I've lost a dime, but made a dollar as a result. I've done all right."

"Is that some macho male kind of deprecation? I thought men liked to boast of their prowess."

The only prowess he'd like to boast about right now was sexual. The thought stunned him. He didn't think of Rennie in a sexual manner. She was helping him find a wife. She was the go-between, not a candidate. She didn't fit his ideal wife at all. She wasn't particularly tall. Her hair would never be considered sleek, and sophistication was just a word to her. She probably slipped off her shoes in church!

Yet he couldn't forget how soft and warm her skin felt. Couldn't forget the merry dancing lights in her blue eyes.

Maybe calling her hadn't been such a good idea, after all, he thought, shifting in his chair.

"Marc?"

"I'm still here."

"When did you want to get together? Let's not discuss this while we have lunch with Marcella. She's got tons of money and would love to invest it under your direction. But I think you ought to wait before suggesting investments to her until you marry her, if she's the one. I want my business situation kept confidential."

"I never mix clients' portfolios," he said stiffly, a bit uncertain whether this Marcella was going to be the right one. Something about the name, he thought.

"Well, that's fine, then. What did you do today, besides make tons of money? Did you quit work early? Marc—are you still at your office?"

"Yes, Rennie."

"That's terrible. Do you realize it's after nine at night? I'm getting ready for bed and have been away from work for hours. I can't believe you're still there. For one thing, you'll ruin your eyes with all that reading. And for another, how do you get dinner? Or do you eat around midnight. That's not good for you to eat and then go to bed."

"I might have left earlier if you'd been home. I've been trying to reach you since seven."

"Oh. Well, I was out."

He remained silent, wondering who she'd been out with, where they'd gone, what they'd done.

"It wasn't a real date or anything, just dinner with a friend. Actually he wanted it to be a date, but I didn't. I just wanted to catch up on news and see him. But you know how men can be. Of course you do, you are one."

"Did he try something?" A dark anger took told.

"No, of course not. He wanted to go out dancing after we ate. I'm wearing slacks, what kind of dork would I look going dancing with a guy while I'm in slacks. I mean people might have trouble telling which was which."

"Better than going out dancing with a woman," Marc murmured, wondering who the man had been.

Rennie laughed. The sound was light and full, and reminded Marc of her eyes, how lights seemed to sparkle from the blue depths. He could imagine them half closed as she laughed, wearing that trifle lopsided smile.

"Cute, Marc. I didn't realize you had a sense of humor. I always think of you as some macho stud. Ruthless, swashbuckling your way through the financial district like a pirate of old. You'd have made it big on the Barbary Coast, and thrown fear into all the gamblers."

"You've thought about me?" he murmured. "Since when?"

"I saw your pictures in the paper a while back. But I don't want to talk about that. How about Saturday?"

"For what?"

"To get together to talk about my books. I'll be glad to tell people that I work with Marc Foster, he handles my business accounts. Think how I can impress—"

"Saturday's out," he interrupted.

"Oh? Why?"

"I can't make Saturday. How about Sunday?"

"Sure. No. Wait a minute. Sunday I have a barbecue to attend at my aunt's house. Come with me. I can bring a date. You wouldn't be a date, but you could come with me and we could talk on the way. It's Keith's mother, my aunt Patty, maybe you know her already?"

"Yes, I do." It had been several years since he'd seen

Keith's parents, but they'd always welcomed him in their home.

"Then you'll fit right in. Only this is casual. Do not wear a suit!"

"I know how to dress."

"Well you couldn't prove it by me. This will be a casual afternoon, one for relaxing and enjoying yourself. And eating. Aunt Patty fixes the best food in the world. She's a much better cook than my mother or grandmother. I wonder where she learned to do that? I don't cook much myself, do you?"

"Just the minimum to get by. What time Sunday?"

"Your car is probably fancier than mine. Can you drive?"

Marc hesitated, then smiled. He enjoyed driving his Mercedes, but he also had something else for Miss Thinks-She-Knows-It-All. "Yes, I'll drive. What time shall I pick you up?"

"About ten. That will get us down there early enough to help set up. We can talk on the way down. It's about an hour's drive."

"I know where Woodside is, Rennie," he said patiently.

She laughed again. "Of course you do. But if things really go well with Marcella and you two make other plans for Sunday, we can meet some other time. I won't mind. And I won't tell anyone you're coming, that way if you don't, no one will think you bagged out at the last minute."

He'd almost forgotten the planned meeting at Friday's lunch. But no matter how much he felt Marcella might fit his requirements, he wouldn't pass up on Sunday with Rennie. He wanted to hear her explanations about her books. And to see her sparkling eyes again.

"I won't make other plans," he said firmly.

CHAPTER THREE

MARC paused in the entryway to the restaurant. He kept his expression neutral, but grimaced inside. The place looked like a restaurant women liked. He'd asked Rachel about it before leaving his office and she told him it specialized in pasta dishes and salads. With the flowers and plants hanging around, he felt like he was walking into a damned garden. He didn't need all the latticework and white wrought-iron furniture, but supposed it appealed to something in the female psyche. Scanning the large floor area, he noted at least a half dozen men, but the majority of the customers were women.

He spotted Rennie in the far corner. Weaving his way through the tables, he kept her in sight as he moved to join her. She still reminded him of sunshine. She had subdued her hair somewhat today, tying it back in some sort of arrangement. Soft golden tendrils framed her face and his fingers itched to brush them away. Did it feel as silky as it looked? If he brushed it back, would the curls entwine themselves around his fingers, as if they didn't want to let go?

He couldn't help risking a peek at her feet. Shod today. The long, dark slacks tapered around graceful ankles, and the silk blouse was a light pink, which enhanced her coloring.

He glanced at the woman seated beside her. Flashy popped instantly into mind. She wore her hair short, better to display the sparkling diamonds swinging from her ears, he thought cynically. The diamond tennis bracelet that encircled her wrist glittered as she waved her hand around in emphasis.

Just as he reached their table, Rennie looked up.

"Why, Marc, what an unexpected surprise. How are you? What are you doing here?"

"Hello, Rennie." He wanted to tell her to cool the surprise and enthusiasm a bit before Miss Diamonds caught on that this was not a spontaneous meeting.

"I planned to meet a friend for lunch, but appear to have been stood up. I saw you across the room, so thought I'd stop by and say hello," Marc said easily. Subterfuge obviously came more readily to him than to Rennie.

"Would you like to join us?" She turned to the sleek woman beside her, "You don't mind do you, Marcella?"

"Not at all." Marcella smiled warmly at Marc, her eyes taking in his expensive suit.

Rennie quickly made introductions and signaled the waitress that they needed another menu. Once the meals had been ordered, she beamed at her two companions.

"This is great, Marc. I haven't seen you in ages. Marcella, you know Marc is a good friend of my cousin Keith's."

"I didn't know that, but I feel as if I already know you, Marc. I've seen your picture in the paper on numerous occasions. Always in the business section, I might add," Marcella said, her eyes almost hungry as they studied him.

"Marc works very hard, that's why he's such a success," Rennie said.

Marcella looked amused as she exchanged glances with Marc. "I assure you, Rennie, I know how successful Marc Foster is."

Marc leaned back and studied the woman Rennie had brought. On the surface she appeared to be exactly what he ordered. She made small talk easily, yet wasn't afraid to show her interest. As the meal progressed, however, Marc became irritated to notice he didn't care one way or another about Marcella Randolph and her opinions.

"Do you enjoy the opera, Marc?" she asked as she ate daintily, pushing the salad around on the plate rather than take a healthy bite.

Rennie looked up. He noticed she'd been eating like she hadn't had food in a month. First a salad, then a large plate of linguine. The sourdough bread disappeared at an alarming rate. Yet she remained as slender as a reed. How did she do it?

"I'm sorry, Marcella, you asked about the opera?" Marc said when Rennie frowned at him and nodded her head toward Marcella as if prompting him.

"I asked if you liked opera?"

"No."

Rennie raised her eyebrows. "That's it, Marc, just no? Why not? I think some of the best operas have been performed by the San Francisco Opera Company. *La Boheme* was a wonderful rendition last season."

"I don't care for opera," he said.

"Oh." She looked blankly at Marcella. "Any of the arts?" she asked.

"The symphony is fine. I enjoy good music, but not people singing in a language I don't understand."

"My parents have season tickets to the symphony, perhaps you'd care to join us some evening," Marcella said, her smile polished, her eyes displaying interest.

Marc smiled. "Perhaps. I, too, have season tickets."

"Imagine that, you two have probably attended the

same symphony performances and didn't even know each other. Now you do,'' Rennie said brightly.

Her smiled looked a trifle desperate, Marc thought cynically. Was she concerned about something?

"Marcella is a big 49er's fan, aren't you, Marcella?'' Rennie said when the silence had stretched out several seconds.

The woman shrugged. "I used to be when we were in school. I think I've outgrown that fascination with football now. Though men never seem to, do they, Marc?'' she said archly.

He shook his head. "Apparently not. I'm still an avid fan.''

"Season tickets, I assume,'' she inquired.

"Of course.''

"Isn't that nice?'' Rennie said. "Maybe you can make up a group and we can all go see a game.''

"Perhaps.'' Marc knew his holding back was annoying Rennie. But he refused to commit himself to Marcella Randolph. On the surface she seemed to meet most of his requirements, but there was something about her that did not quite gel with what he sought for the mother of his son. Three times she'd mentioned her father's money. He might not mind giving unlimited carte blanche to his wife but he didn't want her bragging about it.

When he'd finished eating, Marc caught Rennie's eye. "Glad I ran into you today, Rennie. Thanks for inviting me to join you both for lunch. Marcella, it's been a pleasure.'' He rose and leaned over Rennie, deliberately dropping his head until he could feel her breath on his cheek. If the scene looked intimate, so much the better. He wanted to make sure Marcella had no illusions about any follow-up calls from him.

"I'll pick you up at ten on Sunday, be ready," he said loudly enough for Marcella to hear. With another polite smile at Marcella, he straightened and left.

The startled look on Rennie's face had been priceless. Smiling as he walked back to his office, he wondered how long it would be before he heard from her. He was sure there would be a lecture in this for him. Rennie had surprised him at lunch with her reticence. Obviously she knew how to be quiet when the occasion called for it. But if she had hoped to have Marcella outshine her, she'd mistaken the situation.

For a moment he wondered if she had deliberately brought the most inappropriate woman she knew to lunch. But that didn't sound like Rennie—she was too forthright. She probably thought Marcella fit what he wanted. And on the surface, at first, he'd thought so, as well. But a few minutes in her company sufficed to show the error in that. She'd bored him. As he waited for the elevator, he was startled to realize he would probably never grow tired of listening to Rennie.

Of course he was beginning to know her, and like her. Much as he liked Keith. Maybe knowing she was his cousin made the difference. Knowing she was not at all what he wanted in a wife, he could relax around her. There were no hidden agendas. She would help him out, in exchange, he would hold off closing down her business.

"Marc, you have an irate caller on line one, but she refuses to give her name," Rachael announced midafternoon.

He smiled in anticipation. He knew he could count on Rennie. Even after such a brief acquaintance, he knew enough about her to predict her reactions to certain situations.

"Thanks, Rachel." He pressed the appropriate button. "Hello, Rennie," he said.

"How did you know it was me, I didn't tell your secretary who I was. I didn't want to give rise to gossip, but I should have walked over there and beat some sense into that thick head of yours. Marcella was definitely interested. Aren't men supposed to know the signs? I expected you to ask for her phone number at the very least, although I can give it to you if you like. On my way back to work I realized that asking her out while I was sitting there might have been a tad awkward, but honestly, Marc, saying you were picking me up on Sunday made it sound to Marcella like there is something between us. She asked if she'd be poaching—"

"Rennie, take a breath and let me get a word in edgewise," he ordered.

There was silence on the line. A fuming silence, to be sure.

"I didn't ask for her number because I have no intention in asking her out. And if she thinks we have something going, all the better, she won't pester me," he said ruthlessly.

"Pester? Marc, I thought you'd like her. She's sophisticated, pretty, elegant. Her family is old, old San Francisco and has tons of money. She went to all the best schools. Marcella doesn't have to work, her father settled a huge trust on her. She wears clothes to die for, and has scads of friends. Gets invited to all the in parties and social events. Gives half of them. What more do you want?"

"For one thing, I don't want someone constantly bragging about her father's wealth. I didn't know whether I was supposed to match him dollar for dollar, tell her I could buy and sell him tomorrow, or be impressed.''

''Oh.''

''And I didn't like the way she cut you out of the conversation. I want someone a bit more gracious.''

''Gracious. Good grief. All right. Maybe Marcella is a bit too much. She and I aren't really friends, just acquaintances. Prior to lunch today I hadn't seen her in ages. When you talk to people at parties, you don't have to spend much time with them. But she beats Suzanne.''

''We agree on that.''

''I can't ask anyone else to lunch until sometime next week,'' she said.

''I'm a patient man.''

''Right, I can feel that patience oozing out of you. That must explain why you are such a success, you *patiently* wait for things to happen. You never grab someone by the throat and shake them up, do you?'' Her voice dripped with sarcasm.

''I might grab you by the throat next time I see you, especially if the next candidate is as unsuitable as Marcella. What are you doing tonight?'' he asked.

''I've got a date.''

''With whom?'' Marc didn't stop to analyze the surge of emotion that coursed through him. He gripped the receiver tightly, a scowl on his face. Who was she going out with? Someone she'd known a long time, or a new man?

''You said you didn't need a mother, well I don't need a big brother. You don't have the right to question my dates. I've agreed to help you out, but that's all. Our two lives are separate. Besides, you wouldn't know him even if I told you his name. He doesn't run in the same circles as you."

"Tell me his name, Rennie. It's a simple question, simply curiosity." Marc heard the edge in his voice, but he didn't care. He wanted to know who she planned to see tonight.

"Ha! If the phone company didn't use such strong cable, the heat across this line would have melted the connection."

He clamped down on his furious retort and took a calming breath. "Rennie, I just asked whom you were going out with."

"Joseph Thurmond Sanger the Fourth. Does that make you happy?" she said in a rush, anger coloring her tone.

"And who is he to you?"

"A good friend. A very good friend. Maybe one of the best friends I've got. And maybe after tonight he'll be an even better friend. An intimate friend, if you know what I mean. Not that it is any of your business, Marc Foster. I'm trying to get you a date, you don't have to worry about me finding dates. I have more than I can manage. I've got to go. See you Sunday."

The connection was severed before he could reply. With suspect calmness he replaced the receiver. Someone needed to teach her to stop hanging up on him. Standing, Marc prowled to the window, his dark thoughts focused on Joseph Thurmond Sanger the Fourth. How long would it take to find out who the man was, and what his relationship to Rennie was? His true relationship, not the lover she'd implied.

Sunday Marc donned well-worn jeans and comfortable black motorcycle boots. His shirt was Western in style, and a bit faded from dozens of washings. Because the day looked warm, he left the top two buttons unfastened. Rolling up his sleeves until his forearms were unencumbered, he stood before the mirror. Gone was the sleek businessman he normally saw. In his place was an image of the poor boy from the Tenderloin. Jeans were ubiquitous across class lines, yet he remembered when that was all he had to wear, torn and faded as they'd been. Today he'd be right in style. He'd seen a lot of teenagers wearing ripped jeans, but he could not find it stylish, it brought back vivid, painful memories of the grinding poverty from his childhood.

But no matter what his feelings, he knew how to blend in. Today was casual, he'd go casual. He was comfortable in this attire, even if it reminded him of the past.

He checked his gold watch and noted the time. He'd arrive at Rennie's a few minutes early, go up and wait for her in that frilly apartment. And find out about her date on Friday. He'd thought of little else yesterday when he should have been thinking more about the boys he'd been with. Going through the motions of pickup basketball games, or shooting pool with the older boys, his thoughts had centered around Rennie all day. He already had an image of Joseph Thurmond Sanger the Fourth. Tall, thin, but athletic. The only son of old family money. Attended the best schools and without raising a finger could command the adoration of impressionable young women. Scowling at his thoughts, Marc turned to head for Rennie's.

Standing before her apartment door twenty minutes later, he wondered how long she'd keep him waiting as he rang the doorbell. Somehow she hadn't struck him as the epitome of punctuality.

Rennie swung the door wide.

"Hi, Marc, you're early." She leaned against the door for a moment and let her eyes wander down his body. The tingling awareness he felt around her sprang to life, as did a certain part of his anatomy that he wished would not.

"No traffic." He crossed inside before she noticed anything.

"Come in," she said a bit testily to his back. The door closed with a decided slam.

Marc turned and studied her, from her springy curls to the snug pullover T-shirt that outlined that slender body like a second skin. He wanted to lick his lips when he dropped his gaze to her hips. The jeans she wore were taut over rounded flesh, and he itched to touch the denim to see how tight those jeans were stretched. He looked up into her eyes and felt that same lightness he'd experienced the first time around her. Her eyes danced with humor and happiness. Her smile warmed him and welcomed.

"I'll just be a minute." Was her voice softer than usual? He couldn't tell, only knew it sounded hesitant. If she were truly angry about his pushing in, she would have said something. One thing about a sassy woman, you always knew where you stood.

"You are going to wear shoes, aren't you?" he asked as his eyes followed her down the hall, her bare feet making no sound on the carpet.

"Of course. I'm almost ready. Have a seat."

She disappeared and Marc wandered around her small living room, looking at the pictures on the walls, shaking his head again at the blatant romanticism of the woman. She was in for a rude awakening some day, he thought. Better to contract a kind of business marriage like he planned and forget all the hearts and flowers stuff.

"Ready." Smiling gaily, Rennie rejoined Marc. She carried a small purse with a long strap, which she slung over her head and across one shoulder. The strap nestled between her breasts. Tennis shoes clad her feet. When he looked at them, she laughed softly. "I'll take them off at Aunt Patty's but I'll wear them until I get there."

Leaving, Marc waited while she locked her door, then headed for the parking space he'd found in front. He stopped by his shiny black Harley-Davidson.

Rennie looked at the motorcycle then looked at Marc. He smiled slowly at the puzzled expression in her eyes. Catching her off guard buoyed his spirits.

"Never underestimate the opposition."

"Wow, I never thought you'd own a motorcycle. I almost expected a limo."

"I thought it too pretty a day to waste in a car," he said easily, relishing the knowledge that he'd thrown her off base. Unfastening the two helmets, he handed her one. "This will keep your hair from blowing all the hell."

She drew it on, her eyes big as saucers. "Well, you are full of surprises, aren't you? I would never have expected this. Not in a hundred years. If not a limo, I thought your tastes would run to a Porsche or a Lotus or something outrageously fancy and expensive. But this, wow! Do you know how to drive it?"

"This is outrageously fancy and expensive, for a bike. And of course I know how to drive it. Didn't anyone ever warn you against stereotyping people?"

Rennie shrugged and snapped the chin strap.

"Ever ridden one of these before?" he asked as he snapped his own strap.

She shook her head, eyeing the machine with scarcely concealed excitement.

"You'll like it." The way she threw herself into things, she'd probably end up offering to buy it by the end of the day.

He straddled the big machine, and patted the seat behind him. "Climb on, Rennie."

She swung her leg over and sat gingerly in the deep leather seat.

"Scoot forward and hold on to me," he instructed as he turned the key. The powerful machine roared to life as Rennie pressed herself against him, gripping around his waist with hands that trembled slightly.

"You're not worried, are you?"

He felt her shake her head against him.

"I've been riding bikes since I was a kid. Only transportation I could afford for a long time. We'll be perfectly safe," he promised.

She relaxed her grasp a fraction.

Hell, if he'd had any idea the torment riding double with Rennie would put him through, he'd have ordered a limo for today and sat as far from her as possible.

Her scent swirled around them, strawberries and woman. He knew once they started the breeze would waft the scent away, but as he moved slowly out into traffic, it filled his senses.

Her thighs pressed against his, her arms hugged him around his waist, and her firm breasts flattened against the muscles of his back. For a moment he wondered what she'd do if he turned around, draped her thighs over his and pressed those delectable breasts to his chest. The thought caused a certain portion of his anatomy to harden. Dammit, he had to change this line of thought before something happened that he'd regret. She was Keith's cousin, for heaven's sake. A flaky, bouncy, sassy, unconventional woman who was about to lose her business unless he allowed her to keep it. And the payment was a bride of his own—not a toss in the hay with Rennie.

Though he was tempted.

If he didn't think Keith might kill him, maybe he'd make a play for her—just to while away the time until he found his bride.

It was a pipe dream. He wasn't the type to take advantage of a woman, no matter how tempting she proved. But for a few seconds, he let his imagination roll.

"Hang on," he growled, angry at himself for the salacious thoughts that pooled in his mind, and for the traitorous reaction of his body.

He roared out into Chestnut Street. Heading for the beach, he prudently kept to the speed limit.

"This is great," Rennie said in his left ear.

"I thought we'd go down Highway 1 to Half Moon Bay then cut over. It's a pretty drive along the ocean."

"Great."

She snuggled closer and they were off.

Marc never had a trip fly by so fast. He alternated between keeping track of the traffic on the road, and imaging pulling off somewhere and kissing the daylights out of his passenger. He pushed the big bike to the limit, swooping on the curves, opening the throttle on the straightaway—yet always keeping the machine under strict control. He would take no chances with Rennie's safety. She could trust him in that matter.

And in the other, too. She was not his type. She wanted love and devotion and everlasting happiness when she committed to a man.

He knew that kind of emotion didn't exist for him, but he could offer stability and respect to the woman he married. He'd have to find someone for whom that would be enough. Someone who would advance his social standing, assure his continued access to the important families in San Francisco. Rennie might be fun for a few days, but she was neither sophisticated nor sleek. More rounded and soft, and...

And it didn't matter a damn. She was not what he wanted.

When Rennie said something, Marc turned his head a bit, trying to hear her.

"What?"

"It's hard to talk," she yelled.

He nodded.

"Thought we were going to discuss my loan."

He shrugged, liking the way her body moved against his. "We'll have to talk later."

"Not at the picnic. Aunt Patty won't allow business discussions at her parties. We'll have to mingle with everyone there. Maybe this wasn't such a good idea," she said.

"Why not?"

"I don't want to give anyone the wrong impression."

"Tell them we're friends."

"You're friends with Keith. We hardly know each other."

"I don't know, after the other evening in your apartment, I know quite a bit about you. Your favorite color is pink, you like Louis L'Amour books, you hate tomatoes—"

"This is not a date," she yelled.

"How was your date Friday night?" he asked, reminded by her comment.

"Fine."

He waited. Usually Rennie talked thirty words to his

one. She had little to say on this subject, however. Was it because the date had been wonderful and none of his business? Or had it been the date from hell and she didn't want to talk about it?

"Care to elaborate?" he asked when she remained silent.

He felt her shake her head against his back. "I don't kiss and tell," she said primly.

Jealousy pricked him. He tightened his hands in frustration. *She kissed the guy?* Who was he and what did he mean to Rennie?

"Glad to hear that, in case we ever want to try it," he ground out, wanting to find the man and beat him silly. He still remembered a few tricks from his youth.

He felt her shift against him. "I don't think that would be a good idea," she said.

It would be a dumb idea, he thought. The last thing he needed was any involvement with a woman bent on romance and happy-ever-after.

But he couldn't help thinking about her body wrapped around his, and her lips on his own. She wouldn't kiss and tell, and he wouldn't, either. But he bet there would be plenty to brag about if they ever did.

Marc knew the way to the Hazelwoods' house and didn't need Rennie's pointing out where to turn. But he kept quiet, letting her give the direction.

He hadn't visited Keith's parents' home in over a decade, but it looked as he remembered when they arrived. The gardener kept the plants trimmed and controlled. The lawn was a pristine green, manicured within an inch of its life. The old stone house looked fresh and clean with its windows sparkling in the sun.

Marc pulled into the driveway, maneuvering around

the cars already parked along its length and wound his way up near the house. Stopping, he cut the engine.

He took off his helmet and shook his head, feeling the breeze blow through his damp hair. It was warmer here on the peninsula than in the city. The tall trees near the house and behind it would offer much needed shade.

"That was great!" Rennie said. She reached around him and offered her helmet. "I can't wait for the ride home. We'll have to leave before it gets cold, though," she said. Holding on to Marc's shoulder, she swung her leg over and stood on the ground beside the motorcycle.

He rocked the bike back onto its stand and swung his leg over, standing beside Rennie, crowding her just a bit. One step and he'd be pressed up against her. But he stayed where he was, watching her as she ran her fingers through her hair, trying to bring some of the spring back after being crushed by the helmet.

His fingers itched to touch that hair, and he gave in to the impulse, reaching up and tangling his hand with hers, until the soft curls curved around his fingers— catching hold just like he'd thought it might.

She went still, staring up at him with her pretty blue eyes, emotions changing as quickly as lightning. Slowly he pulled her closer, his hand tangled in her hair, his eyes holding her gaze as the distance between them narrowed. He would taste those lips again, and not with a slight brush like the last kiss. This time it would be hot and wet and deep and long. He would open her mouth and learn her taste and touch. He'd bring that sexy body up against his and make her forget kissing last night's date.

Marc noticed the flush to her cheeks, the way her lips parted slightly as if she were having trouble breathing. His heart kicked in hard and the desire between them couldn't be hidden. Her heat and his mingled, banished only by the slight breeze that cooled his skin. Slowly he drew her closer.

"Marc Foster! I thought I recognized that motorcycle. It's good to see you again." Patty Hazelwood hurried down the walkway from the front door, a wide smile of welcome on her face. "And Rennie? I didn't expect you to come with Marc. Or I guess it's the other way 'round, isn't it?"

At the sound of the voice, Marc dropped his hand and took two steps back. Standing to his full six feet two inches, he took a deep breath. Two seconds later and Patty Hazelwood would have found her niece locked in his arms.

"Patty, good to see you again." He held out his hand, but she brushed it aside and gave him a quick hug. Then holding his arms like he was her son, she studied him.

"Let me look at you. It's been years since I've seen you. Keith keeps me up-to-date, and of course we read about you all the time in the paper. You look tired."

"That's because he works all the time and never takes time off for recreation, to pump up the creative juices. I told him that he should keep regular hours," Rennie said.

She kept her aunt between her and Marc, and by the nervous way she wiped her hands on her hips, Marc knew she'd been disturbed by their close call. He smiled grimly. It wasn't over. He'd kiss her before the day was done.

"I'm working on that," he said, nailing her with his gaze.

"We're working on it, wouldn't you say?" Rennie challenged.

"Something I should know about?" Patty asked, picking up on the undercurrents.

"Marc's advising me on my business. We were supposed to discuss it on the way down, but it's hard to carry a conversation on a motorcycle."

"Or when you can't get a word in edgewise," Marc murmured.

Patty laughed. "Rennie does tend to rattle on, doesn't she? Come on, you two, let's get into the backyard. Keith's here and Myra and Becky. I expect your folks will be here before long, Rennie."

"We came early to help set up, if you need it," she said, walking up the walkway, every once in a while throwing a nervous glance toward Marc.

"We can use the help. Marc, go on through and see what Keith needs. You come with me, Rennie."

Marc nodded and headed for the backyard. Though it had been years since he'd visited, nothing had changed.

"I wonder if I could get the same results trying to boss him around," Rennie said, deliberately loud enough for him to hear as he cut through the family room out to the patio.

Marc swung around and caught her making a face at his back. "Want to try?" He raised one eyebrow.

She opened her mouth as if to meet his challenge, then shook her head and hurried after her aunt.

He watched her go, an easy sight in those tight jeans and top that hugged her figure.

"Hey, Marc, what are you doing here? Good to see you." Keith joined him at the door.

"I brought Rennie."

Keith's surprise was almost comical. "You brought Rennie? What's going on?"

"We had some business to discuss. I couldn't make

it yesterday. She suggested we do it today.'' Marc didn't often explain things to others. He'd passed that stage years ago and saw no reason to start with Keith.

''I see,'' Keith replied, clearly puzzled. ''You two strike a deal?''

''She introduced me to Marcella Randolph on Friday.''

''Good.''

''Not so good. Marcella isn't what I'm looking for. Do you know a Joseph Thurmond Sanger the Fourth?''

''Joe? Sure, his family and ours have known each other for years. Why? Did you come across him recently?''

''What does he do?'' Marc had no intentions of telling Keith why he wanted to know. He could put one of his employees on the trail, but maybe Keith would offer a shortcut.

''He's a doctor. Works at Seton Medical.''

Keith's father joined the two men, greeting Marc and catching up on business and the subject of Joseph Thurmond Sanger was dropped. But Marc knew a bit more than when he'd started. For the rest, he'd find out one way or the other. Starting with Rennie!

CHAPTER FOUR

MIDAFTERNOON Marc grabbed a glass of iced tea from the picnic table and dragged an Adirondack chair into the shade near the patio. Settling in it, he let his gaze wander around the yard. It was crowded with friends and family of the Hazelwoods. He'd met everyone, and remembered each person. It paid to remember names, he'd learned that when he first started in business. Some of today's guests he'd known when he had visited Keith during college, others were new to him—like the Quackenbushes. Rennie's mother was very much like Patty, likable and friendly. Theo Quackenbush obviously adored her, and his stepdaughter.

Marc took a long pull of the tea. He'd helped set things up, kidding with Keith and his father. He'd carried out platters of food for guests to nibble on until time for the barbecue dinner. And unable to help himself, he'd met every new arrival wondering if it would be Joseph Thurmond Sanger. The Fourth. At one point, unable to stand the suspense, he asked Keith if the man was expected. Mixed emotions met Keith's explanation that Joe had to work. Would he have come if he hadn't? Would Rennie have attended the party with Joe instead of himself if the doctor hadn't been on call?

And if he had? Marc had no claim on Rennie. She had invited him because she thought they would discuss her financial records on the drive down. It didn't matter. She had invited him, and he was here, not Joseph Thurmond Sanger. The Fourth. Marc was the man who would take her home tonight. And get some answers about what the other man meant to Rennie. The emotion that churned in his chest suspiciously resembled jealousy.

Patty and Keith Senior welcomed him, questioning him earlier about what he had been doing and offered sincere congratulations to his success.

"He likes being top dog." Rennie said in passing. Her friendly, sunny disposition could almost be construed as flirting. But she was friendly to everyone, even the man threatening to take away her business.

As the afternoon wore on, Marc felt more and more like an outsider. The other guests played tennis on the court at the end of the grass, or horseshoes on the far side. The children frolicked in the free-form pool, screaming and yelling their delight with the day. He watched almost enviously. It was a far cry from his own childhood. A far cry from the way some of the boys he knew lived now. Wouldn't they give their back teeth to enjoy such an afternoon?

He made a mental note to explore taking some of the older boys swimming the next time he went to help out.

"Too much?" Rennie asked, dragging a wooden chair over and plopping down beside him, stretching her legs out before her. One glance confirmed she'd long ago discarded her shoes.

"Too much what?" he asked, turning slightly so he could see her. He'd watched her since they arrived, still aware of the kiss they'd almost exchanged, still wanting it. She'd greeted everyone with a hug or a kiss, asked about what was going on, listening with every evidence of fascinated interest. Maybe he should go out and come in, that would get him a hug at least.

"Too much noise, commotion, racket. I don't know.

It can get overwhelming sometimes, I think. Maybe not for the parents of the children, they are used to chaos, but the rest of us are more sedate in our activities. This is pure unleashed exuberance. Can you imagine starting your morning early, running everywhere, screaming at the top of your voice, and then having enough energy to go swimming?''

He nodded, smiling slightly. ''Somehow sedate is not an adjective I would normally associate with you.''

She laughed. ''Well, maybe sedate isn't the right word. But I wondered if you were looking for an escape. Though I guess you'd just walk through the house and out the front door if you were.''

He raised an eyebrow. ''Oh?''

She nodded, her eyes dancing. ''Sure. I can see you intimidating everybody, never having a qualm about doing whatever you feel like doing at the time.''

''Based on your vast knowledge of me.''

''Based on your arrogant, don't-give-a-damn attitude, most of the time,'' she replied easily. ''Actually, I doubt if anyone would even notice for a while. There must be seventy-five people here. Aunt Patty loves to have friends and family over. I think she should have had a dozen babies instead of only Keith and Gloria. Of course if she'd had more boys like Keith, I'm not sure the rest of the world would have survived.''

''Keith is a friend of mine,'' he reminded her lazily.

''And mine, now,'' she promptly returned. ''But I can remember him from when I was a kid, and he was a terror. He's almost ten years older than I am, he should have been taking care of me, not driving me crazy. Of course, he's mellowed with age.''

''He's not that old.''

She looked directly at Marc, her smile caused him to

catch his breath. He wanted to kiss her, here, now, and forget about the crowd in the yard, the women gossiping, the men bragging. What would they all say if he reached out and dragged Rennie into his lap and covered that sassy mouth with his own?

"Why, Marc Foster, I do declare, I plumb forgot that you are as old as Keith. Of course that puts you right in your prime, isn't that what you said?" she teased.

"Someone should have paddled your backside when you were little."

Laughing again, she studied him, amusement evident. "Lighten up, Marc. This is a fun-filled afternoon and here you sit on the sidelines, watching instead of participating. Or are you planning your own parties when you marry that paragon of sophistication that we're going to find you? I'm sure Aunt Patty isn't the least bit concerned with being sophisticated. But are you enjoying today, or would you rather we all dressed up and sat quietly sipping white wine?"

"If I marry, it doesn't follow that I would move to Woodside. I like living in the city."

"Ah, but don't you want a huge yard for your kids to roam around in? I would expect you'd want them to have every advantage—learn tennis and riding, swimming and dance. Golf lessons at the country club. Fess up, you plan to give them everything money can buy, don't you?"

"Are you badgering my favorite boy?" Patty Hazelwood asked as she strolled over to join them.

"Whoa, Aunt Patty, what about Keith?" Rennie asked, patting the arm of her chair for her aunt to use.

"Well, he can be a bit tiresome, but Marc was always the perfect guest. We've missed seeing you these last few years," Patty said, perching on the arm of Rennie's chair. "You don't have to wait for an invitation, nor for Keith to bring you. Stop by sometime and keep us up-to-date with your life."

Marc nodded, but remained uncommitted. He'd always felt the welcome from Keith's parents, and always made every effort not to abuse their hospitality. He was too conscious of the vast difference in their backgrounds. Not that they had ever hinted at any disparities. The visits he'd made when in college had whetted his appetite for the finer things. Their house was warm and welcoming, even with its understated wealth. It was the kind of home he wanted. But ever conscious of his background, he would not intrude.

"Good luck, Aunt Patty. The man works all the time. If I want to call him, I know now to try work first. Even if it's nine o'clock at night. Honestly, he needs a keeper."

"What are you doing calling him at nine at night?" her aunt asked, clearly intrigued.

Rennie blushed. Marc watched, fascinated, as the color rose from her throat, flooding into her cheeks, tinting them the most delightful shade of pink. This was the nineties, it was not uncommon for women to call men. Yet the embarrassment was clear. Was there a hint of old-fashioned values in Miss Rennie Morgan? He grew even more interested in this complex woman.

"Actually, it was business," Rennie mumbled.

"Business?" Patty asked, glancing between the two of them.

"I'm taking a look at her books," Marc explained, unaccustomed to the surge of protective instinct. "I asked her for some more information and she tried to reach me at home, only trying the office as a last effort." He threw away the words, as if they meant nothing. No point in getting Patty Hazelwood thinking anything was going on between them. Especially when there was not.

"And what were you doing there at nine? Don't tell me you are turning into a workaholic. There is too much else to enjoy about life," Patty admonished.

"I enjoy my work," Marc said, torn between amusement and amazement that Patty seemed to be scolding him.

"I love my work, but know enough that it will be there the next morning. I leave it behind and return refreshed the next morning. If you work constantly, you get used up," Rennie said. "You need a hobby."

His eyebrow rose again. "Such as?"

"I don't know. Want to give horseshoes a try?"

"I'm sure the people who live below me would be thrilled."

She laughed. "Not at your apartment. Now. The alley is free and we could play. I bet you have never even tried it."

"Go on and give it a shot, Marc. I'll get Keith to come give you some pointers if you like," Patty said, rising.

Rennie jumped up and reached for Marc's hand. "Don't you dare, Aunt Patty. It may be the only time this year I can beat someone at the game. Come on, Marc, I'll teach you what you need to know."

Marc waited by the motorcycle while Rennie finished saying goodbye to everyone. It was later than they'd planned to leave, but after dinner the conversation had been enjoyable. Neither of them paid any attention to the time. It would be dark soon. And it was growing cool. He had a leather jacket in the bike's compartment, he could let Rennie wear it.

She burst from the front door and ran down the steps. "Sorry to keep you, I had to talk to Sally Eberhart for a moment. And then Mom insisted I get a sweater for the ride home." Shrugging into the oversize sweater as she hurried, she continued talking. "Uncle Keith is lending me this one. It's wool, so supposed to keep me warm even though it's not very thick. Of course I should have told them I could snuggle up to you and keep warm that way, but—" Her head popped out of the neck and she came to a halt, gazing straight into Marc's eyes.

He waited for the next bit, wondering what her mother had thought of her snuggling up to him. Knowing he would enjoy the sensation. Maybe he should yank that sweater off and let her put plan two into action.

"You can snuggle anytime you want," he said.

She swallowed and licked her lips. He wanted to taste those lips, to feel that delightfully feminine body press against his. To draw her close and capture her energy, hold it for as long as he could.

"Just on the ride home, thanks." She seemed flustered and he smiled in grim satisfaction. She jarred him off center, time it happened to her. He pulled on his jacket, glad for its warmth. As he kicked the bike off its stand, he thought about their game of horseshoes. She'd laughed and cheered when she scored, muttered dire imprecations when he did. Yet he couldn't remember another time he'd enjoyed an afternoon so much. She had drawn him in and banished the feeling of being outside, never giving him another opportunity to sit alone on the sidelines. It was a gift she shared with her aunt. He wondered if she knew how rare it was.

They rode straight up Highway 280 into the city, skirting the neighborhoods and shopping centers along the way. The lights of San Francisco glittered in the early autumn night, illuminating the tall buildings that soared against the black sky.

"I love the city at night," she said as they rounded the curve and it lay before them, the Bay Bridge outlined in white lights to their right.

"It looks like a fairy-tale place, doesn't it?" she said in his left ear.

"Looks like downtown to me."

"That's romantic."

He laughed. The woman was in for a rude awakening if she thought to ever find a spark of romance in him.

"Do you have time for a quick cappuccino?" Marc asked as the motorcycle slowed for a stoplight. He didn't usually stop in these trendy coffee places, but knew women liked them. He'd heard plenty about one near the office from Rachel.

"Sure. It's not that late, and I'm still keyed up from the party. Doesn't Aunt Patty throw wonderful ones? I haven't laughed so much since the last one she gave. But I don't think I could have stood much more of Bobby and Stephie Jenkins. If they had argued over one more thing, I would have gone screaming into the night."

Marc chuckled, remembering the two teenage siblings who couldn't agree on anything. If he had a sister or brother, would they have bickered constantly? Or been close, like Keith and his sister?

The coffeehouse was quiet, only a few customers scattered at the small tables. He ordered cappuccino for both of them and followed Rennic to a table near the back wall. It was isolated and quiet. A restful respite after the hectic afternoon.

"We never did get to talk about my business. I loved riding on your motorcycle. Can you believe I'm twenty-six and never rode a motorcycle before? It was so much fun, I might be tempted to get one myself. But practically speaking, if you'd driven a car we could have discussed what your accountant discovered while we rode. I mean, that is why you came with me today, right?''

Marc stalled by taking a sip of the hot coffee. He couldn't remember why he'd said yes to her invitation, only that he had wanted to spend the day with her. The books were only the excuse he'd used. Not that he'd admit that to anyone.

''I have questions and comments Stuart jotted down. We'll have to make time to go over everything. And I still need your checkbook, to check the entries.''

''Let me check my calendar and get back to you. Maybe we could do lunch,'' she teased, taking a sip of the fragrant coffee. ''Mmm. This is so good. You did get decaf, didn't you? I can't be up all night and I'm wired enough from today that it'll be hours before I can sleep as it is. Anyway, I have some work to do when we get home. I thought we'd be back earlier. But at least I have enough energy to get going. It's sample favors for a wedding I'm planning. Sometimes having the actual product for the bride-to-be to hold in her hand helps in the sale.''

''I ordered decaf.''

''Thanks. I should have known you would. You strike me as the type to do exactly what you say every time. Did you have a good time today?'' she asked.

''I did.''

Blinking, she grinned. ''Careful, Mr. Foster, you might spend a few more words than you can afford. That's it—I did? Would you care to elaborate on what you enjoyed the most? Was it the food, the man-talk by the barbecue pit, or the patter of little feet? Wait, I know. It was learning how to play horseshoes!''

"Learning how to try to interpret your version of the rules, you mean. If I thought I'd play again, I'd get a book with the official rules." *But you are what I enjoyed most.* His gaze skimmed over her tousled blond hair, the flush of color on her cheeks, the brightness in her pretty blue eyes. Resting on her lips, he wondered if he would taste the cappuccino if he kissed her now. He'd wait. They'd be at her apartment soon. Time enough then to indulge in the craving that had surfaced that morning and not yet been assuaged.

"We might not have talked about my financial records, but I came up with another idea of someone for you to meet. Julie Treherne," Rennie said triumphantly.

"Julie Treherne?" Marc placed his cup carefully on his saucer and looked up.

"It came to me when we were discussing kids. Julie loves them. And that is the primary reason you want to marry, right? She volunteers at Children's Hospital and works each Christmas on the toys for kids programs. Her mother is not from the Bay Area, but her father's family came with the gold rush. She might just be the perfect choice. And we know she loves kids so she'd be a great mother.''

For a moment Marc hesitated. Why, he refused to consider. He nodded. "So you can arrange an introduction."

"Same as before, if you like."

"Let me choose the restaurant this time," he said dryly.

"Not into salads and pasta?" she asked, her eyes dancing in amusement.

He wanted to bottle that look, take it home and be able to take it out anytime he wanted to be cheered up.

She had such a freshness about her that made him feel centuries older, and eons more cynical.

"I felt like I walked into a damn garden."

"Okay, we'll try something more masculine. How about the London Pub over on Kearney?"

"When?"

"I'll have to call you once I set something up with Julie."

He took another sip of the fragrant brew. "Tell me something, Rennie. Do you plan to get married sometime?"

"I hope so. I want what my mother and father had. What Mom found again with Theo." She flashed her grin and shrugged her shoulders. "I know, you think I'm hopelessly romantic, but I don't care. I want love so strong I never feel alone again. When it comes, I want to feel bonded for life to one man. And then I want lots of kids. I'm an only child, you know. I loved visiting with Keith and Gloria, even though they are older than I. They had each other, but I had no brothers or sisters. I wished Mom and Theo had a few, but they never did."

Marc remembered her brief background Keith had reported. After the death of Rennie's father, it had only been she and her mother for a number of years. They shared that bit of similarity, though she didn't know it. Only her childhood had taken a turn for the better when Theo Quackenbush married her mother. His had continued, solitary, lonely, poor. No new mother came into their home, it was just he and his father.

"So what will you do with your dozens of kids?" he asked, shaking off the gloom of memories.

"Cut back on work, for one thing. I missed my mother so much when she had to go to work after Daddy died. So I'd arrange for Eve or someone else to take on more responsibility and I'd spend time with my children. We'd go whale watching in spring, and to the zoo. Did you know sometimes you can get a night pass and go in after dark? All the animals look different after dark. It's spooky, but a lot of fun—as long as you remember a flashlight! Then we could go backpacking in Yosemite, or explore all the little shops in Chinatown.''

''And would you send them to the school you attended?''

Rennie wrinkled her nose. ''Probably not. It was fine, and Theo really wanted me to go there. Mom had gone and Aunt Patty and Theo's sister, so it was sort of a tradition. And I got a good education. But I also enjoyed the local public school when I went, probably would have received just as fine an education. Did you go to private school?''

He shook his head, dark amusement lurking. ''About as far from some fancy private school as you can get,'' he answered, memories of his high school days not something he cared to dwell upon.

''There, see, you turned out fine. I think San Francisco has a great public school system, so my kids would go there.''

She looked up from beneath her lashes and held his gaze, hers teasing. ''I don't think our kids would interact too often, would they? I don't plan on lessons on every activity from ballet to archery. I don't plan on some ritzy, snooty private school. If they want to learn something, I'll be supportive, but I'm not one for forcing things down people's throats, and especially not a child's.''

''I want more for my children than I had,'' Marc said. ''I want to offer them the best that money can buy. I have the resources and plan to use them. No child of mine will ever want for anything."

She blinked and stared at him. "Excuse me? You sound like you plan to buy your children everything they ever ask for."

"Right."

"Great way to spoil them and have them grow up expecting the world at their feet. Which it won't be."

"They'll be mine to spoil. I can afford to buy anything."

"Marc, children don't need lots of *things*. They just need love. A child will develop into a far better adult if he has love and attention from his parents. A strong home so he'll know he is safe and wanted and loved. Toys and such are fine for treats, or special events, but you sound as if you plan to just throw things his way."

"Of course he'd have attention. My wife won't work, she'll stay home with the children. I'll be home nights and weekends."

"You'll have to change your habits," she murmured.

"Think I wouldn't?"

"I guess you would, if that was what you wanted. I have to get home now. This has been a wonderful day. Thank you for coming to Aunt Patty's with me."

He rose and reached for her hand, lacing his fingers through hers. Her skin was soft, her fingers strong, yet small when compared with his. She didn't pull away, but held on as if holding hands was something they always did. For the first time Marc wondered what it would be like to be friends with Rennie Morgan. Forget about his threat of foreclosing on her business, forget about her finding him a bride, just take the time they had together and enjoy. He'd never had a woman friend, and wasn't sure it was possible. But for a moment he was willing to try.

"So I'll check with Julie and call you. Any day this week okay with you?" she chattered as they headed for the bike.

"If I see a conflict, I'll call you."

"Okay. I'll try for early in the week."

When Marc reached her apartment house, she slid off the bike before he cut the engine.

"Thanks for taking me today." She held out her helmet.

"I'll walk you to your door," he said, removing the key and snapping off his helmet.

"I'm sure I'll be fine."

"Probably, but I'll still walk you to your door."

Somewhere between the coffee shop and her apartment, her warmth had cooled. He didn't try to reach for her hand, but quietly followed her up the steps in the old building to the second floor. Waiting patiently while she fished out keys from her snug jeans, he resisted the urge to sweep her into his arms and kiss her until morning.

"About your books—" he said.

She glanced up warily, and looked adorable. Unable to resist temptation that had plagued him all day, he reached out and cupped her chin in one hand, lowering his face until her sweet breath brushed across his cheeks.

"What about them?" Her eyes deepened in color, and a hint of pink swamped her cheeks.

Marc liked the effect. He wondered how often he could provoke a blush.

"We need to spend some time together to review them. How about one night this week?"

"Fine. You're the one who stays at work until all hours. I normally leave around six."

"I'll call you." He leaned forward the scant inch that separated them and closed his lips over hers. He slid his hand around until it cradled her head, his fingers tangling in the soft silky hair. The starch evaporated and Rennie made a soft sound in the back of her throat as she leaned against him, her fingers clutching his arms. He deepened the kiss, holding her close, reveling in the sweet sensation of their embrace.

Endless moments ticked by as they were lost in a world of sensuous haze and delight. Slowly reality returned. Marc ended the kiss, resting his forehead against hers as he looked into her bemused eyes.

"I'll call you," he repeated.

"Okay. That's fine." She licked her lips, looking stunned. "I'll be home most nights. So whenever..." Her voice trailed off and she moved one finger to trace his lips, pulling back to see him clearly.

"I'm not sure kissing me is getting much accomplished."

He released her. "What do you want to accomplish?"

"Finding you a wife so you'll back off foreclosing on my business."

He stepped back, feeling as if he'd been slapped. "I haven't forgotten our agreement, Rennie. You do your part and I'll live up to mine."

Without another word, he turned and left. Seething at the way she'd changed the flow of the evening, he wanted to punch something. How dare she complain about their kiss? It was no big deal. Most men expected a kiss after a date. It wasn't as if he pushed her into bed. Not that the thought didn't come to mind, lurking in the recesses to distract his attention, his focus. He was on a wife hunt, and needed Rennie to help. Their relationship was solely business. So why the anger at her comment? It was nothing but true. Her purpose now was to introduce him to a possible mate. In exchange, he'd forgive the business loan.

It was a sensible arrangement.

So why did her kisses tempt him so much? Why had he considered making an attempt at friendship? Why did he want Rennie so much when she was totally opposite to his picture of an ideal wife?

He needed to make sure she remembered their deal and moved ahead. Rennie didn't impress him with her business acumen, nor speed in closing a deal. Maybe he needed to push her a bit. As soon as he found his ideal bride, he could turn over Rennie's loan papers and move to the next stage of his life.

He sat on the bike and looked up at her windows. The light was on, but the shade drawn. He couldn't see her. And he couldn't erase the echo of her words. When she married it would be for love. Nothing less.

He kicked the bike on and eased the throttle. Pulling onto the main street, he opened the throttle and sped toward his own condo in the marina. Love was an illusion, a fancy term for lust and affection and commitment. He would not be seduced by the illusion. When he married, it would be with both eyes open, and with a commitment on both parts for a lifetime marriage.

CHAPTER FIVE

MARC entered the London Pub just before noon on Tuesday. As promised, Rennie had called and left a message with Rachel that she and Julie would be meeting for lunch today. He arrived a few minutes early, in hopes of spotting them as they came in. Maybe he could make a snap judgment about this Julie and if she didn't appear to suit, he could forgo lunch with another woman who compared her father's wealth to everything else.

The decor was that of an old English pub. Dark paneled walls polished to a high gloss reflected the brass lamps that hung from the ceiling, which, along with the wall sconces, provided the illumination for the restaurant. The chairs were solid, the tables of dark wood. Marc had eaten here a time or two before. He liked the quiet elegance, the quick service and the illusion of privacy. The tables were not crowded one against another to pack in the customers. The owner preferred quality over quantity. And the patrons paid dearly for the dining experience.

He felt a surge of pride that he no longer worried about the cost of things. It was a far cry from the struggling times of his youth. Scanning the large dining area, he spotted Rennie and a petite dark-haired woman just taking seats. Obviously they arrived even earlier. Was he typecasting women—thinking they were always late? He frowned. He needed to be able to read people in order to succeed in his business ventures. He didn't want prejudices to interfere.

He started for their table.

"Can I help you, sir?" The maître d' stepped in front of Marc, his silver hair gleaming in the muted lighting.

"I am joining the ladies over there." He nodded toward Rennie's table.

"They made no mention of expecting a third party." The maître d' obviously took his role seriously.

Marc looked at him. "Rennie Morgan is the blonde, and she is expecting me. Perhaps she neglected to mention the fact when being seated."

Obviously torn, the man hesitated a moment. Then, after a quick glance at Marc's Armani suit and expensive silk tie, conceded defeat. Marc smiled cynically. Look and act the role and people will accept it without question. It was a maxim he'd learned years ago.

"If you will follow me." The man took off through the tables, his bearing upright and stiff.

Damn! Marc didn't want the maître d' involved. How spontaneous would it look with the man leading him directly to their table?

"Madam, your third party has arrived." The maître d' stood stiffly by the table, eyeing Marc as if he were a suspected pickpocket.

"Oh." Rennie looked up at Marc, at the maître d', and then cast a quick glance at Julie.

"You've been more than helpful," Marc growled at the maître d' as he slid out a chair and waited for Marc to be seated.

"Oh, Marc. Won't you join us?" Rennie said, looking at the chair the maître d' held.

Marc sat down and glared at Rennie. If she had other ideas of how to meet prospective brides, she'd better come up with them fast. This was the last time he'd pull a stupid stunt like this.

"Uh, Julie! I'd like you to meet Marc Foster, a friend of mine." Rennie looked flustered.

Marc almost smiled at the picture. Once again he was struck by Rennie's lack of guile and subterfuge. He nodded to the pretty dark-haired woman seated to his left.

"Julie?"

"Julie Treherne, I'm happy to meet you. Were you and Rennie supposed to meet for lunch? If I'm in the way, we can reschedule our lunch." She looked at Rennie, a question in her eyes.

"No, of course not, Julie. I wanted to have lunch with you. I—" She stared in Marc in supplication.

"I often eat here, Julie. When I arrived and saw Rennie, I thought I'd stop by and say hello. Our friend at the door didn't seem to understand," Marc improvised, ruthlessly maligning the maître d'. "I'm really the intruder. If you'd rather, I can sit at another table." It would probably prove a better idea, he thought, thoroughly disgusted with the entire situation.

"No, of course not, Marc. Do stay. Will that be all right, Julie?" Rennie said breathlessly.

"Sure. You know I have to leave in a bit, anyway. I'm working this afternoon at the hospital and don't want to be late."

"Right. Julie works at Children's Hospital," Rennie said brightly, her gaze fixed on Marc. Some of the worry faded, but she still looked flustered.

He nodded and picked up the menu, striving for some normalcy.

"She loves children," Rennie added.

He flicked her a glance. She looked stressed. Turning to Julie, he smiled politely. "Have any of your own?" he asked.

Rennie yelped and shook her head, her curls dancing.

"Marc, Julie isn't married," she explained as if to a two-year-old. She glared at him.

"What a coincidence," he said, holding Rennie's gaze. He liked her flustered. He didn't remember seeing her like this before. "I'm not married, either."

"Oh, God." Rennie rolled her eyes, and reached for a glass of water. Sipping desperately, she looked at Julie.

Marc also looked at Julie and liked what he saw. She was dainty and petite. Her hair was glossy black, worn in a casual cut that would be easy to care for. Her clothes were stylish without being ostentatious. And there was not a single piece of jewelry in sight. He wondered what her father did, and if she knew his net worth to the dime.

"Tell me about working at the hospital," he said, taking pity on a decidedly nervous Rennie.

Julie instantly plunged into recounting every experience she'd found working with children. Marc listened with half an ear as she droned on and on about some child who had proved a terror while in the hospital and how she'd been instrumental in calming him down; about another boy who almost single-handedly wrecked the X-ray equipment at the hospital until she stepped in to save the day. Stories of relieving overworked nurses, of rocking fretful babies until they cooed with happiness, of bringing treats and reading stories to the demanding toddlers who depended on her to soothe their stay grew old fast.

He flicked a glance at Rennie. She sat still as stone, a silly grin plastered on her face, her eyes glazed slightly as she kept them firmly fixed on Julie.

Ordering lunch only halted the monologue temporarily. After ten minutes, Marc mentally apologized to Rennie for ever thinking she talked nonstop. He'd give anything to hear her interpose a few words. To hear anyone else say something for a few minutes.

Lunch arrived, and Julie at last became quiet.

While the silence stretched out, Marc reviewed his requirements for a wife. Obviously along the way he'd neglected to mention he liked conversation, a give-and-take between adults, not a monologue. He'd have to refine his list.

"Marc has season tickets to the 49ers," Rennie blurted out.

Both of her table companions stared at her.

"Right?" she asked.

"Yes." Marc pressed his lips together to keep from smiling. Rennie obviously didn't like the quiet that had enveloped the table. What would she say next? While he might enjoy conversation, he had no more patience with inane remarks than monologues.

"Roger works for the 49ers," Julie said.

"Roger?" Marc asked.

"My cousin, Roger Jackson, he works in the office."

"I didn't know that," Rennie said brightly. "How interesting. Isn't that interesting, Marc?"

His lips twitched. "Very interesting."

He laid down his fork and leaned back, watching Rennie, trying to guess what she would do next.

"Uh, Marc attended Stanford with my cousin Keith."

He almost smiled. Ever the trouper, his Rennie.

"My cousins Beth and Rolly both went to Stanford. Of course Jack and Roger went to Berkeley, so that always causes lively discussions during Big Game Week," Julie replied.

"You seem to have a big family," Marc commented.

"I guess, let me see…"

Stifling a groan when she started naming the members

of her family and their occupations, Marc had no one to blame but himself. After her discourse on the hospital, he should have known she'd be able to go all night with her family. And as he tried to keep the names and relations straight, he realized she really did have a large family. And seemed totally in awe of each one, quoting their words as if they were gems.

At a pause, he pushed back his chair. "Sorry not to be able to hear about the rest of your clan, Julie, but I have to get back to work."

"Oh, look at the time. I didn't realize. I'll be late at the hospital. They do depend on me so much. I hate to be late. Do you want to share a cab? Rennie, it's been great. We'll have to do it again real soon. I'll call you." Julie pushed back her chair and stood, smiling at Marc.

Her expression quiet with satisfaction, Rennie looked from one to the other. "Lunch sometime would be fine."

Marc didn't like that look. And if Julie thought by leaving at the same time he'd share anything with her, she was sadly mistaken.

"Rennie, shall I drop by tonight, or would later in the week be better?" Marc said, moving to her side and leaning over slightly as if implying a degree of intimacy. Actions spoke louder than words, and as with Marcella, he didn't want Julie to have any wrong ideas about their meeting.

"Tonight?" Rennie looked blank.

"About eight." He brushed his lips across hers and straightened. "I'll walk out with you, Julie, but I don't need a cab. I'm only a couple blocks from my office and can walk."

Marc settled into his chair, his jacket flung across the back, and drew the latest figures from the proposed joint venture between rival factions in the Silicon Valley from the stack of folders on his desk. An awareness of anticipation hummed beneath the surface. He knew from Rennie's shocked expression that she would not ignore his farewell. How long before she called and blasted him to kingdom come?

The door flung open and slammed against the wall. Marc looked up, and almost smiled. No more phone calls.

"You can't just barge in like that." Rachel stood beside Rennie as if considering whether dragging the intruder from her boss's office was a possibility.

Rennie ignored her, her eyes latching onto Marc. She stomped across the carpeted floor, fury radiating from every inch of her. Tossing her purse onto a visitor's chair, she glared at Marc, her hands on her hips.

Marc placed the prospectus on the desk and nodded at Rachel. "It's all right, Rachel. I'll deal with this."

Once the door closed behind her, Rennie exploded.

"You'll deal with what? I thought you were serious about trying to find a wife. I've been racking my brains for days trying to come up with that perfect paragon you want and each time I present someone who would suit, you act like a damn idiot and try to make them think there is something going on between us!" She slammed one fist on his desk.

He wondered if it hurt. Her fist wasn't so big and the desk was massive.

"I thought we agreed to pretend the meetings were spontaneous, unexpected. Instead, you have the maître d' come over and say I was expecting you. I couldn't believe it. How can I pretend anything is spontaneous when you are announced like that? We're just lucky

Julie left with you instead of staying to cross-examine me!''

She paused and took a breath.

''Not only that,'' she continued before he could open his mouth. ''I can't believe you kissed me in public. Do you have any idea what kind of impression that would make on Julie? Not only that, but did you know Steve Crawley was sitting two tables away? He's a good friend of Theo's. I can just imagine his comments to my stepfather. 'Say, Theo, old man, didn't know little Rennie was involved with a man.' 'What man?' Theo will ask. And then Steve will tell him about the entire sordid scene and Theo will remember you were at Aunt Patty's and soon the entire family will think there's something between us and we know there is nothing!''

She turned away and stormed to the window. Marc watched her, trying to gauge her anger. Was she truly furious, or was there something else simmering beneath the surface? After a moment, she turned and stormed back to the desk.

''Well, aren't you going to say anything?''

He shrugged. ''What's there to say? Julie is not what I'm looking for.''

She rolled her eyes and flopped down into the chair across from him. ''A simple 'It was nice to meet you, Julie, goodbye,' would have sufficed, don't you think? But no, you have to go on and deliberately tell her you would be dropping in at my place later. I bet Steve heard that, too. Oh, great. Now my mother will be on me trying to find out why I haven't mentioned you before and getting hurt feelings that she and I are not as close as we once were. When of course we are, because there's nothing to tell about you and me. I certainly don't want the family to know I'm having trouble with the business.

They would all jump in and insist I take a loan. I wanted to make it on my own. Damn!'' She jumped up.

Marc looked at her. Was she shorter? Rising slightly, he glanced at her feet. Her shoes were lying on their sides, obviously kicked off.

''Anyway, what's wrong with Julie? She's pretty, very polished, and loves kids. The perfect mate. Or as perfect as you're likely to get.''

He leaned back in his chair and watched her pace his office. Her eyes were darker than he'd ever seen them. Her cheeks a rosy blush of anger that caught his eye. He wondered if her skin felt warmer with that color. Wondered if he could kiss her out of her anger. Not likely.

''First, Julie is pretty, but a bit short for me, don't you think?'' he asked calmly, belying the increased heart rate as he watched her turn and walk back toward him.

''How short is too short? She's not much shorter than I am. Am I too short? You never mentioned anything about short or tall. I thought you wanted sophisticated and impeccable bloodlines. You never mentioned height as a requirement. I would have remembered if you had.''

Rennie was just the right size, he thought whimsically. The top of her head came to just above his shoulder. He had to lean over a bit to kiss her, but when he'd pulled her into his arms, she fit perfectly.

''I want sophisticated, but a certain height would be preferred. Do you want me to get a permanent backache leaning over to kiss my wife the rest of my life?''

She frowned, staring at him as if something unexpected had been said. Taking a breath, she looked away. ''That's it? You're afraid of backaches?''

''No. Did you notice how every story she told about the hospital reflected on how wonderful she was to be volunteering? What a heroine she is in every scenario? I wonder how the place runs without her," he said dryly.

Rennie looked out of the expanse of windows. Slowly she walked over to them and leaned against the sill, gazing at San Francisco.

Marc thought he caught a glimpse of a smile in her reflection.

"You're right. She did come across as the heroine of every event. But at least she likes children. Family's important to her. I thought you wanted that."

"She sounds as if she's related to half of the city. And if she quoted one more relative, I would have gone crazy. Doesn't she have an original thought in her own mind?"

Rennie looked at him over her shoulder. "I thought men liked that, having the woman parrot their every thought as if they were a god or something."

"If a man's looking for a life partner, he wants someone who can think for herself. Otherwise, it would be like talking to myself. And that's another thing. She talks nonstop."

Rennie smiled at that. Marc felt the now familiar clutch at her lopsided grin and his entire office brightened. It was as if sunshine invaded the somber room. Slowly he rose and crossed the room to stand beside her by the bank of windows.

"She did tend to get carried away. But maybe she was nervous. You are rather an intimidating presence," she said.

"I've never noticed you are particularly intimidated."

"Well, you're a friend of Keith's. Almost a cousin, you could say."

"Don't start listing all your relatives and quoting them," he warned.

She laughed. "Don't try to turn the subject, Marc. I'm still mad at you."

"Why?"

"For one thing, you didn't give Julie a chance. I think she's just what you are looking for. She would make a good wife, and wouldn't want to work. She loves her volunteer job. Working around that when the kids come would be an asset."

"I didn't like the way she bragged about it. I volunteer but don't have to make myself the center of attention."

"You do? Where?" Clearly intrigued, Rennie turned to face him, her face alive with curiosity.

He frowned. He hadn't meant to say that. Few people knew about his activities with the center and it suited him to keep it that way.

"Marc, where do you volunteer?" Her hand came out and touched his arm. He could feel the heat through the fine cotton of his shirt. Slowly he looked at her. She was waiting patiently, a decided contrast to the rampant curiosity that blazed in her eyes.

"We are discussing Julie Treherne, not my personal life," he said coldly.

"We'll discuss Julie in a minute. Right now I want to know where you volunteer. Is it with old people, children, the sick? I can't believe this. Most men like you say they have too little time to volunteer regularly. Oh, I suspect that's what you meant. Especially in the same sentence with talking about Julie's regular schedule."

"Let it go, Rennie."

"I won't. Tell me."

He hesitated, then nodded once. "I work at a center for boys in the Tenderloin—a couple of Saturdays a month. It's not such a big deal."

"The Tenderloin? You actually go into the Tenderloin?"

She couldn't have expressed any more surprise if he'd told her it was on the moon. The Tenderloin was one of the poorest sections of San Francisco. There were stories of gangs and shootings and drugs. As far from the elegant surroundings of his Montgomery Street office as she could possibly imagine. "Why in the world do you volunteer there? There are other boys' clubs in safer neighborhoods."

He nodded, once.

"How in the world did you even find out about the center, much less get started working there?" Rennie was clearly baffled. Marc wondered if she were trying to envision her cousin Keith or some of her friends doing that. Impossible, probably.

He smiled grimly. "I am from the Tenderloin. It was sort of like going home."

She stared at him, dropped her gaze to his expensive shirt, the costly tie, the discrete gold watch at his wrist. Slowly her gaze moved back up until it collided with his own.

"Not fit the image you had?" he asked. For some reason her answer was important.

"How long did you live there?" she asked.

"How long? I grew up there, Rennie. My old man was a dock worker, when he could stay sober enough to work. Otherwise he just took whatever odd jobs he could to keep us in food and liquor. I left when I won the scholarship to Stanford."

"And never looked back."

"My father is dead. My mother left when I was little. No need to look back."

"But you go there now to volunteer?"

"You wouldn't understand."

"I might. In fact, I bet I do. You had a...a sparse childhood, and now you have a ton of money. You want to do something for the kids still living there."

"Sparse?" He laughed, shook his head. "Only you would call abject poverty *sparse*. But I was lucky, I got out. Now I'm trying to make sure some of the others can get out, too."

"I doubt it was luck. You seem to make your own luck. And I'd say hard work and lots of studying got you into Stanford. And got you where you are today. But it sure explains your demands for a high-society wife. Marc, you can't erase the past by marrying into some other family."

"So my roots will always show?" He raised one eyebrow, narrowing his eyes. "What are you trying to say— that I'm not good enough for the fancy wife I want?"

"No, I didn't mean that." She looked horrified. "I meant, finding the bloodlines you want isn't everything. You should be tremendously proud of all you've accomplished. I know you want to leave your fortune to a son, but don't shortchange yourself in the process. Don't marry just to make sure your son would never end up in the Tenderloin. What about you, Marc, don't you want more? You should hold out for love."

"Oh, God, Rennie, don't give me that. I know you think love surrounds everyone, and maybe it does surround you. Or maybe you see things in such rose-colored glasses that you can believe in such nonsense. But in real life, I'm not sure it even exists and I don't plan to live my entire life searching for something that doesn't exist."

"Your way of finding a wife is so cold-blooded."

"But it is my way, and it suits me. I don't want my

son to be ashamed of his father, or long for a mother he never knew. I want him surrounded by stability and financial security. Marriage is a merger of two lives, and something to be entered coolly and logically. We wouldn't have so many divorces today if everyone took a bit more time to fully consider every aspect before getting married. The illusion of love doesn't last.''

"I don't believe that." She sighed, and looked back out the window. "I'm not sure I can help you."

"You'll help me or lose Brides and Bows." A split second of panic touched him before he snapped out the words. They had a deal and everyone knew he held all participants to every term of a deal. Was she attempting to renege?

"You have to do your part. Maybe you should invite Julie on a date.''

"Give it up, Rennie. If I couldn't stand lunch with the woman, there's no way I'm going to want to spend the rest of my life with her."

"Just what do you want? I've introduced you to two people I thought would work, based on your list of requirements. Both are pretty, stylish, rich, come from San Francisco's finest families. Neither work, both would stay home with your children. Both would be an asset in spending your money. What else?''

"I don't know. There's just something missing." Maybe it was that neither woman brought sunshine into his life. He was aware of Rennie, standing inches away. Her scent wafted gently in the air, teasing his nostrils. She stood in her stocking feet, her softly draped blouse concealing as much as it revealed. The long light wool pants did nothing to remind him of her jeans on Sunday. He rather thought he liked the snug jeans better.

"You might have to ease up on some of your requirements," she said slowly.

"Like what?"

"I know some women whom you might like, but they work. And I can't call them up and ask them if they plan to work once they have children. But if it comes up in the conversation, I'll pass it along."

She tilted her head and stared up at him. "Want to give that a try?"

Her expression was wistful, her eyes deep and luminous and mesmerizing. Marc felt he could stare into Rennie's eyes all day. Except he'd rather kiss her.

Without further thought, he leaned across the distance that separated them and did just that.

She didn't move. Didn't step closer, didn't pull away. For endless moments his lips caressed hers, and she responded. Then Marc straightened.

"What was that for?" Her voice sounded throaty, soft, bemused. Almost caressing, he thought in disgust. This deal was unlike any other business venture. Was he getting soft in his old age? Next time he'd stick to businessmen who dealt in dollars and cents, not soft women with rosy views of life and silky skin that tantalized and taunted him to touch, to feel, to taste.

"Friends?" he offered. The idea of being friends grew with every meeting. Of being more than friends.

She blinked and drew in a deep breath. "I guess."

"I don't want to meet for lunch with the next candidate."

"What then? That is so easy."

"You can think of something, I'm sure."

"If you want, I could fix you up with someone and not be there. A blind date?"

"No. You have to be there. If I need an out, I can use you."

"Fine, use me then. But unless I give a party or something, I don't know of many ways to be in the midst of an introduction. Oh, wait, I know of a party. I received the invitation a couple of weeks ago. I wasn't going, but maybe that would be the answer. You can come as my date. I'll introduce you to everyone and you can decide who you want. Why didn't I think of this earlier? It would get it all over with at once. It's Toddy and Denise's anniversary party. Practically everyone we went to school with will be there, married and singles alike. As will a range of other people. They always have hordes attending. It's perfect. It's a week from Saturday."

"I volunteer at the center on Saturdays."

"It doesn't start until seven or eight at night. You can work all day at your boys' center and then party all night. I'll have to scrounge around for the invitation. I don't remember what I did with it. I hadn't planned on going. But it would be the perfect opportunity for you to meet several women at once. As soon as I find it, I'll call you and let you know the details. This is perfect!"

Marc considered the alternatives. He wasn't much for parties, but it was a way to meet women without giving rise to unrealistic expectations. "All right."

"But this is the last try. You have to find someone from this group. I don't know anyone else," she warned.

"Then I'd better fulfill my part of the bargain. Did you want me to come by tonight to go over your records?"

"Oh, I forgot." She turned and hurried to her purse, which she had tossed in the chair. Rummaging in it for a couple of seconds, she waved a checkbook triumphantly. "I remembered. I meant to give it to you at lunch, but forgot with everything else that was going on."

He took it from her and slapped it against the palm of one hand. "Tonight, Rennie?"

"I won't be home tonight. Besides, you need to look at the checkbook first, don't you?"

"Why won't you be home?" Everything inside him went still. Was she going out on a date?

"I'm meeting Joe for pizza and a movie. We're going to see that new Schwarzenegger adventure flick. Why is it guys love adventure movies? You'd think a doctor would be tired of all the blood and violence, but Joe loves them."

"Joseph Thurmond Sanger the Fourth," Marc murmured, clamping down on the emotion that started to swell. She was free to date whomever she wished. But why did he hate hearing about it? The emotion churning inside threatened to consume him.

She looked at him warily. "Mostly we call him Joe."

"Blue blood from way back?" he asked silkily.

Nodding cautiously, she watched him as he stepped closer. "I guess you could say so. His family came to California generations ago and has always been very prominent in San Francisco politics. His uncle was the mayor a few years back. He doesn't have a sister, if that's what you're hinting at. Only two brothers. I don't even think he has any female cousins."

"Why are you going out with him?" Rennie wasn't his type. He wanted sophisticated and savvy, not a romantic with an ingenue enthusiasm. But he didn't like knowing she preferred Joseph Thurmond Sanger over him.

"Why not, we're friends." She licked her lips, the wariness giving way to confusion.

"Just friends?" He pushed, he wanted to know more about this relationship, needed to know more. Did Joe kiss her? Did she like his kisses? Want more? Jealousy burned deep in Marc as he awaited her answer.

She nodded.

"How friendly?" He reached out and captured one of her curls, smoothing it around his finger, his thumb registering the soft texture.

"Friends. You know, someone to do something with."

"Are we friends, Rennie? We did something together Sunday, going to the barbecue."

"Friends don't blackmail other friends into helping them," she snapped instantly.

He smiled slowly. "Our deal is not blackmail, that's business. I'm talking about being friends. I've never had a woman for a friend before."

"Somehow I'm not surprised." She licked her lips again, her eyes darting from his to his mouth.

"Rennie, I want you and me to be friends." He leaned over and kissed her again. Lightly, not giving in to the need that built inside to crush her against him and kiss her until the sun set, but nonetheless responding to the silent invitation she issued.

"Uh, sure, Marc. We're friends, I guess," she said when he released her. Color rose in her cheeks again, but he knew it was not anger this time.

"Spend Saturday with me?"

"I thought you worked at the center in the Tenderloin on Saturdays."

"Every other one. I worked last week, but next Saturday is free. Spend it with me." He almost demanded she do so, but caution stilled his tongue. He wouldn't force the issue, unless he had to. But if she had time for her *friend* Joseph Thurmond Sanger *the Fourth,* she could damn well make time for him, as well.

"Doing what?" she asked, taking a step back.

Reluctantly he let his finger slip from her hair, dropped his hand to his side.

"We can decide when I come to your place tomorrow night."

"What?"

"I still need to go over your books."

CHAPTER SIX

"YOU never give up, do you?" Rennie asked, frowning.

"Look on it as protecting my investment."

"Your investment? Brides and Bows is *my* boutique."

"And I hold the note on it. If this party is our last shot and nothing turns up, I'll foreclose. Then Brides and Bows will be a part of Foster Associates," Marc said coolly. He didn't believe in mixing business with anything.

"I've introduced you to two appropriate women," she protested. "It's not fair that you'll take my business."

"That's what we're discussing, Rennie, business. From a logical point, I've already given you more than is justified. My company made you a loan. You have not repaid it. You owe me."

She stuck her feet into her shoes. "I'm doing the best I can," she muttered, snagging her purse and slipping the strap on her shoulder. Tossing her head, she faced him from across the office.

"Come at eight. But don't come in a suit, or I won't let you in."

"Dictating terms?" he asked softly.

"You're darn tooting, Marc. After you have your say about my accounting methods, which I'm sure you will find a total mess, I want more discussion on the qualities of this wife of your dreams. If the party is my last shot for Brides and Bows, I have to make it a success! Eight o'clock, and no suit!"

She made an exit worthy of a stage actress, he thought

as he watched her sail from the office. The door almost slammed, but at the last second Rennie apparently had second thoughts. She closed it quietly. The click when the latch engaged sounded loud as he stared after her, torn between amusement and frustration. He hadn't run the gamut of so many emotions in more than a decade, if ever. Yet around Rennie, he was subjected to a full barrage.

He slapped the checkbook against his palm again and wondered why he was willing to put up with so much from her. If his mother had remained, would his parents have had more children? Would he have had a sister like Rennie? Not at all likely, not living where he'd grown up. Children there acquired a hard edge early. They didn't live with a rosy view of life, they faced reality as babies. Rennie would never survive in such a place. And he hoped she never even visited.

Marc called Stuart to come for the checkbook and finish his analysis of the records for Brides and Bows. The accountant sighed softly when handed the checkbook but made no comment.

"I want it by tomorrow at five," Marc said as dismissal.

"No problem, boss. At least I hope not. You'll have everything on your desk before five."

Marc glanced at his watch. It was scarcely three. He had over twenty-nine hours before he'd see Rennie again. Time he needed to spend on work, not on thinking about a blond fireball who set his emotions churning.

Promptly at eight o'clock the next evening Marc rang the bell to Rennie's apartment.

The door opened a crack and he saw Rennie peek out at him. Smiling broadly, she threw the door wide. "Hi," she said, her eyes running appreciably down his body, taking in the casual brown slacks he'd worn with the cream pullover shirt.

"Looking good, Mr. Foster," she said, stepping back so he could enter.

"Relaxed enough, Ms. Morgan?" he asked.

"Admit it, you feel better in those clothes than in a suit and tie."

Not that he would admit it, but he felt better seeing her. Enough that he'd done as she had requested and worn casual attire, he wasn't going to give her the complete satisfaction of agreeing with her.

"Ready for business?" he asked.

Sighing, Rennie nodded, motioning to the small alcove where she had her dining room table and chairs. "Thought we could spread everything out on the table and you can lecture me on basic accounting."

"Lecture?" He raised an eyebrow.

She eyed him through lowered lashes. "Isn't that the purpose of this? I can't imagine my record-keeping is up to your usual standard."

"Let's just say you have an innovative and creative way with accounting like you do with your bridal dresses."

She smiled. "Sit. Can I get you some coffee?"

"If it's strong and black."

"All the better to keep us awake while we go over this?"

"Accounting bore you, Rennie?" From the table, he could see her bustle around in her small kitchen. He wondered how good a cook she was, and if she entertained often. That thought brought others—ones he didn't care for.

"How was your date with Joseph Thurmond Sanger the Fourth last night?" he asked.

Her head swung around and she stared at him for the longest time. Slowly her eyes narrowed. Picking up the cups, she approached the table.

"You know, you could just call him Joe like the rest of us," she said slowly. Placing his cup before him, she pulled back the chair to his right and plunked down. "My date was fine," she said.

"Where did you go?"

"Good grief, Marc, you sound like a jealous husband. We went for pizza. We had fun. End of discussion. You didn't come here tonight to grill me on my date with Joe, did you?"

He shook his head, wondering if he were lying to himself. Dammit, he didn't like the thought of Rennie out with another man. Refusing to dwell on the precise reason for his feelings, he turned to the pile of envelopes and notebook pages before him.

Two hours later Marc wished he'd let Stuart handle this. Torn between exasperation and amusement, he still wasn't sure he'd gotten through to her. Her rationale in her creative bookkeeping could drive a saint into a tailspin, much less a hardheaded, bottom-line-oriented businessman.

"That's it. If you follow those suggestions, I guarantee you'll show a jump in your profit the first month," he said, leaning back and stretching. Lowering his arms, he caught her looking quickly away. Had she been watching him? A gratified satisfaction swept through him. He'd looked at her enough, good to know the shoe was on the other foot once in a while. She was aware of him, as well.

"I don't know, Marc. To demand so much money up

front seems to make the whole business so mercenary, somehow.''

''Mercenary? Rennie, you're in business to make money, right?''

''I guess.''

''You guess? You have to know that much. If this is just a hobby—''

''No, I want to support myself. Just not make a lot of money.''

''Why not?''

''Why?''

''Why what?'' Was he losing the trend of the conversation?

''Why should I want to make a lot of money? As long as I make enough to live on and to pay Eve, that's fine.''

''Your business has to make money to keep you and Eve employed. And why not make all you can?''

''Lots of money is nice, but not necessary to enjoy life.''

''It sure is.'' He knew that for a fact. Never again did he want to be in the position of being as poor as he'd been as a child. Money made a world of difference, from how well a person lived, to the opinion of others.

''So tell me, Mr. Rich Man, how do you enjoy your money? What do you do with your leisure time that uses lots of money? From the little I know about you, you don't even go home from the office at a reasonable time. You volunteer at that boys' club, which isn't exactly leisure activity, it must be a lot of work. I know you have season tickets to the symphony, but how often do you go? What do you spend your pots of money on?''

He reached for the empty coffee cup, looking into it as if it would miraculously give him some answer. When she said the words, he had a hard time coming up with a satisfactory answer. He didn't do much more than work. But he enjoyed that.

"Work gives me a feeling of satisfaction," he said slowly, meeting her gaze. "It's my hobby as well as my career."

"I like my job, too. But I don't need lots of money to enjoy what I'm doing. I just do it."

"One difference between us is that I am not in danger of losing my business because I enjoy my work."

"No, you're too ruthless to let that happen."

"I'm not running a charity, Rennie."

"I don't want charity."

"Then stop running your business like one. It is not unreasonable for you to demand one-third of the cost of the gown at the commissioning, one-third at the first fitting and the balance at the final fitting. That way, you wouldn't have taken such a loss on that dress on the mannequin."

"How do you know about that dress?"

"Eve told me."

She looked away, clearly unhappy with his directive.

"Someone will buy it. It is such a beautiful dress. I love it. It was one of my better creations," she said slowly, defensively.

"It is pretty, no one is denying that. All I'm saying is you wouldn't have taken such a loss if the woman had paid for two-thirds before she decided to cancel."

"I guess."

"And you'll start buying in quantity?"

"When I can afford it," she nodded. "I know that makes good sense, but right now money is a bit tight. As you well know."

"I can lend you what you need. It's foolish to keep

buying one item at a time when even a small multiple order can save you over twenty percent.''

''I don't want to borrow any more money,'' she said stiffly, her eyes flashing when she faced him. ''That's what got me in this mess in the first place.''

''We're not talking a lot of money, not compared to what you already owe me. Look on it as protecting my investment. If you find me a wife, I erase the debt.''

''And if you don't like anyone I introduce?''

''Then Brides and Bows will be in a better financial state when I take it over.''

She balled her fists and leaned closer. Marc felt his heart kick into higher gear and the delight he always felt around her rev up. Now what?

''You can't have my shop. If I have to introduce you to every single woman in San Francisco I will do so. But you have to do your part and make some sort of effort. I can't do it all myself!''

''You're pretty when you're angry,'' he said.

''What?'' Her eyes widened and she sat back in her chair as if stunned.

Marc smiled. For once he'd thrown her off balance. Maybe that was the key, say outrageous things when she least expected it. She did it enough around him, he should take a page out of her book.

''You heard me. In fact, Rennie, I'm surprised you're not married already. When I first met you, I thought Keith had set me up—you know, trying a bit of matchmaking between us.''

''Us? As in you and me? Not in this lifetime.''

''Ouch, and why not?''

''For one thing, I'm not sleek and sophisticated, in case you hadn't noticed,'' she said, tilting her head. ''My mother's family goes back for generations, but my father's—my real father's family—doesn't. He was just a cop. Killed in the line of duty. And I don't have money of my own. Wouldn't you be worried I'd be marrying you for your money?''

He laughed, tilted back on the two back legs of the chair and tucked his fingers into his pockets. "No, especially after your enlightening discussion of earlier. Money is not a primary issue with you. Love is.''

"Damn straight. When I marry, I want a husband who loves me. Who wants to spend time with me, not hang around work until all hours making money. I want someone who takes an interest in my business, who will help me cook dinner, and do his bit around the house. We'd do things together, like go on hikes, or down to the beach. Or just ride the cable cars and people watch.''

"You don't have expensive tastes," he murmured, intrigued to find out what she thought of as an ideal marriage.

"Well, I wouldn't mind going on a cruise," she said slowly, watching him carefully.

"A cruise?"

"Mom and Theo went on one a couple of years ago and loved it. I've wished ever since that I could take one.''

"Lying in the sun, having someone wait on you hand and foot?''

"Actually it was an Alaskan cruise and I was thinking more about all the food I could eat.''

"Especially the shrimp and chocolate?''

She smiled and Marc knew then he wanted to kiss her again. More than when he'd first arrived. More than during the evening when her fingers would brush against his, or when her unique special scent invaded his nostrils. Her smile lightened everything, and he wanted to capture some of that light for himself.

Without thinking things through, he reached out and pulled her from her chair into his lap.

"What—"

His mouth cut off the rest of the sentence. For a long moment Rennie held still, then she relaxed and leaned into him, her arms encircling his neck as she pressed her breasts again his chest. Capturing light and sunshine wasn't easy. But her kiss buoyed his spirits. He truly liked Rennie Morgan. He would miss her when he married and couldn't spend the evenings with her.

Pulling back, he gazed down at her flushed face, her eyes drowsy and soft, her cheeks fused with color, her lips slightly swollen from the pressure of his. She looked adorable. For a moment he wondered if his plan was sound. Maybe he should consider Rennie as his choice.

No—bad idea. She wanted more than he had in him to give. Love, and sharing, and devotion. He wanted a wife who would grace his table, be an asset in business, bring impeccable breeding to their children. He wanted entrée into the finest homes in the city and needed a wife who could provide that. Being allied with a powerful family would go far to cement his place in San Francisco society and business community. The specter of his childhood would be banished forever.

"I have to go." He stood, easing Rennie to her feet.

"Sure. Thanks for the lecture on accounting," she said, clearly confused by his abrupt departure.

"Any time. Do follow some of the things I outlined, it will make it a lot easier to keep track of your exact situation."

"Right, and insist I get paid up front."

"At least enough to cover your expenses if someone decides to cancel at the last minute."

"It was one dress. I won't have any trouble finding someone to love it as much as I do."

"Right." He headed for the door, needing to get some air. He didn't like the feelings that seemed to grow each time he was around Rennie. Jealousy about her seeing Joseph Thurmond Sanger the Fourth. Desire that grew each day. And the uncertainty that was beginning to blossom about his original goal. Damn, he knew better than to get sidetracked once he established his objective. Time to get on track again and get this over with.

"Are we still on for Saturday?" she asked at the door.

He took a breath, and nodded. One day, what could it hurt? And they wouldn't be locked up in her cozy, homey apartment, just the two of them. They'd be outside, surrounded by strangers. "I'll pick you up around nine."

"See you then, Marc," she said softly, her eyes holding a mysterious message deep in their depths.

San Francisco's famous fog covered the city Saturday morning, cool and damp. The day hadn't started auspiciously. Marc wondered what Rennie would want to do in such weather. Nothing appealed much to him. A walk on the beach was out. It was too cold and damp. People watching was probably out, as well, who else would be wandering around in this pea soup?

Even riding his motorcycle was out. Too cold for that. He parked his car two blocks from her apartment, finding no place closer. Knowing his mood wasn't the sunniest, he stood before her door and wondered if he should just cancel the entire day.

It opened before he decided.

"I didn't ring," he said, taking in the bright picture she made. Jeans faded so much from washing they were almost white, but not quite. A pale blue sweater over a dark blue shirt. Her blond hair curled every which way—probably due to the dampness in the air.

"You didn't have to ring. It is precisely nine, and you are always on time." She grinned in triumph and tilted her head. "Want to come in or are we ready to go?"

"Where do you want to go? In case you haven't looked outside, it's miserable."

"Not so, just refreshing and exciting, like San Francisco. We have the gift of a cool day to do whatever we want. Eve is covering the shop, so I'm footloose and fancy free. What's first?"

He scowled at her. Perky had its place. Today was not it. "I had planned to take you on a bay cruise. Not quite like the ocean liners, but a cruise," he said slowly.

"I've never been. That's great."

"We'd see nothing, this fog is right down to the ground."

"It'll burn off by afternoon. Let's do something else this morning and then we can do the cruise thing. I'm ready."

"Grab a jacket, it's cold outside."

In two minutes they were on the sidewalk in front of her house.

"No bike?" she asked, looking around.

"Too cold and damp. I brought my car, but couldn't find a place to park on your street. It's not far."

"I don't mind walking, I like it. Do you ever just walk around the city?"

"Not in recent memory," he murmured, remembering days when walking was his only mode of transportation.

Rennie laughed. "No, I suppose you are too busy to

walk around. You probably take a cab or drive yourself anywhere you want to go.''

''Pretty much.''

''Well, I don't want to just drive in the fog. What did you have planned?''

Marc paused. Damn, he had planned on the cruise. Then maybe lunch somewhere and let the afternoon take care of itself.

''Earth to Marc,'' Rennie said, touching his hand.

His fingers curled around hers and he looked down at her. ''I'm more used to quiet dinners and nightclubs,'' he said.

''Don't you date on the weekends?'' she asked.

''I rarely date at all.''

''Of course, too busy playing workaholic. Time you had a bit of fun, Marc. Especially before marrying your trophy bride and having your two point six children. Shall I make a couple of suggestions?''

''No, I think I can handle things.'' They reached his car and he unlocked the door.

''A Mercedes, now why am I not surprised?'' Rennie murmured as she slid into the leather seat.

''Probably because you wouldn't admit to surprise even if you were,'' he retorted as he sat behind the wheel.

''Powerful, stylish, and expensive, the perfect car for the rising executive.''

''I've risen, in case you hadn't noticed.''

''On the backs of little people like me.''

''Hey, babe, if you want to play with the big boys, you need to toughen up.''

''Ha! Stay out of shark-infested waters, you mean.''

''Did you sign that loan document with your eyes open?'' he asked as he pulled into traffic.

"Yes, but I was dealing with Brad Peterson, and he didn't seem nearly as ruthless as you."

Marc kept quiet. He didn't like the fact she considered him ruthless. Hadn't he agreed to forgive the debt if she came up with a suitable candidate?

"Where are we going?" Rennie asked after a moment of silence.

"Union Square," he said.

"Why?"

"You'll see."

"Tell me about some of your other friends," she said, settling back in the seat and gazing out the window.

"Which friends?" he asked.

"Well, not me or Keith. Others." She waved her hand.

"Most of my friends, as you call them, are really business acquaintances. Except for Steve."

"Who is Steve?"

"Director at the boys' center."

Rennie looked at him closely. "I was teasing when I said you work all the time, but maybe I was closer to the truth than I expected. Do you ever do things for fun, just pure plain fun? Or is everything directed toward building a fortune? I know you had a tough childhood, but don't let that rob you of what you can enjoy now. You've made a bundle, cut loose and enjoy some of it."

"I'm hoping we'll enjoy today," he said stiffly. His life suited him, or had until Keith had thrown him at Rennie. Maybe it had been a mistake. If he had not attended that charity ball with Suzanne, he and Keith would not have run into each other. No, it was more if he'd kept quiet about his quest, this would not be happening.

Glancing at Rennie, he smiled slowly. But he'd miss

today with his new friend. All the aggravation she threw at him was worth today.

"You're going to ride a cable car?" Rennie asked as they joined the queue near Union Square.

"And why not?"

"I can't picture it, that's all."

"What's to picture? I get on, sit down, buy a ticket, get off when we reach Chinatown."

"We're going to Chinatown?" Her eyes lit up and she smiled broadly. "That's great!"

"I remember you saying you'd like to explore every shop in Chinatown," he said as the line moved forward. When a tourist loaded with cameras blundered into Rennie, Marc pulled her closer, turning a bit to shelter her from the pedestrians on the sidewalk. His arm around her shoulder felt good. She snuggled right up against him as if she belonged.

"That's sweet, Marc. That you remembered what I said and planned for us to spend part of the day there."

He nodded, pleased he'd remembered that at the last second. At least prowling the shops in Chinatown would be warm, she wouldn't be out in the damp.

"And we can eat dim sum for lunch."

"What?"

"Dim sum. You do like dim sum, don't you?"

"Chinese food?"

"Lunch, you know where they push the cart around and you pick and choose what you want to eat." Rennie pulled back enough to see his face.

"Sounds fine."

"You've never eaten dim sum, have you? I can't believe it, born and raised right here in San Francisco and never eaten dim sum? Have you eaten on North Beach?

Or do you limit your restaurants to those that populate the financial district?''

"I've eaten at some of the best Italian restaurants on North Beach. And at the wharf, and the top of the Bank of America building. I don't limit myself to the financial district. I just haven't eaten dim sum.''

"It is lunch, you probably can't tear yourself away from work.''

He lifted her chin with a finger and caught her gaze. "No more slanderous comments about my work. We're out here to have fun and I don't appreciate your deprecating my career.''

She blinked. "I'm sorry. You're right.''

Before she could say any more, their cable car arrived. They watched the brakeman and conductor push the car on the turnstile until it faced up Powell Street. Joining the surge of people, they scrambled for a seat. Rennie squeezed in against Marc and turned her shining face to his.

"This is so much fun. It's been ages since I've ridden one.''

"Good," he returned. An unusual feeling settled around his heart. Refusing to give it a name, Marc watched her as the cable car lurched and started up the hill, fascinated anew at her enthusiasm over the most commonplace things.

It was as if it were a day out of time, Marc thought as he and Rennie wandered in and out of the numerous shops lining Grant Avenue. Neither spoke about the past, nor their respective businesses, nor of anything earth-shattering. But every moment was priceless. He loved watching her examine the lace or the carved wooden scenes, then put them down with a gentle smile at the proprietor.

"Want to buy one?" he asked as they regained the sidewalk after one episode.

"Good heavens, no, where would I put it? But they are so intricately carved, I'm fascinated. And the lace is lovely. I might want some for a gown or veil."

"If you don't plan to buy anything, why are we shopping?" he asked.

"We're shopping, not buying. Looking, browsing. Don't you enjoy looking at things, try to figure out how they were made?"

"Not particularly."

"Well, I do. Come on, I want to stop in this one." Rennie took his hand and Marc threaded his fingers through hers. He didn't care if they went into a hundred shops, she was pleased with the day and he had wanted her to enjoy it. Did she do this kind of thing with Joseph Thurmond Sanger?

They stopped for dim sum at a restaurant a block up from Grant Avenue. Crowded with families and couples, it bustled with energy. They were lucky to get a table almost immediately.

Rennie ordered jasmine tea and looked at the first cart that passed their table. "Shall I order things for us?" she asked.

Marc nodded. "Do you know what everything is?"

"Not a clue, just what's good and what I want to avoid. This is pork." She pointed to a steamed dumpling. "They have lots of shrimp items."

"Now I know why you like dim sum."

She laughed. "Maybe you're right. This is so much fun. Thanks for asking me out today," she said.

"I'm glad you're enjoying yourself. Do they have forks at this place?" he asked, picking up the chopsticks.

"I doubt it. We can ask, or you can learn to use chop sticks. I'll show you."

By the time Marc managed to competently transfer food from his plate to his mouth with chopsticks, he felt he could handle anything. It was tedious and treacherous, but he was determined to master the art that Rennie made seem so effortless. Her laughter and joy at his efforts had nothing to do with his perseverance.

"At the risk of sounding like your mother, learning new things is good for you," she said.

He shrugged. "I don't know what my mother would have said. She left long before I could remember her."

The smile faded from her face. "I'm sorry. I didn't know."

He caught her eye and smiled. "No problem, she left when I was small. Didn't like living in the Tenderloin, I guess."

"And your father never remarried?"

"No."

Eating the last bite from her plate she laid down the chopsticks and took a sip of the hot tea. "So founding your own family is very important, isn't it?"

"Yes. And it has to be the right family. I don't want any child of mine to ever question anything. I want him to know his grandparents, to know his place in life. And not to have to..."

"To what?" she said when he fell silent.

"Nothing. If you are finished, want to head for the wharf? If the fog's lifted a bit, we can still get on that cruise."

"I hope you get the perfect wife, Marc," she said gently.

"If not, it won't be for lack of trying, now will it?"

CHAPTER SEVEN

IT WAS after dark by the time Marc brought Rennie home. The bay cruise had been a success, despite the cold wind and the fog that still hovered cold and damp. When they'd returned to the Embarcadero, Rennie discovered Marc had never been to Pier 39 and insisted they make that their next stop. She cajoled him in to buying truffles at the chocolate shop, browsed through the specialty shops that catered to tourists by carrying every imaginable trinket emblazoned with the words San Francisco. They had eaten at a small restaurant specializing in clam chowder and sourdough bread. He had laughed, and argued, and felt more alive than any time in the last few years. No wonder Joseph Thurmond Sanger wanted to spend time with her, Rennie was a delight.

The cable car ride from the wharf back to Union Square sped by. Because night had fallen, lights sparkled from the buildings, muted by the defusing aspect of the thick fog.

"I hope you had as much fun today as I did," Rennie said when he pulled into a tight parking space only two buildings from her apartment.

"I'm glad you enjoyed yourself," he said. "I'll walk you up." Marc wanted to be invited in for coffee. He didn't want the day to end.

"No need to do that, I can manage," she said quickly.

"I want to."

"Oh."

Rennie was unusually silent on the short walk to her apartment. She said nothing as Marc took the keys from her hand and unlocked her door, opening it and waiting for her to proceed him into the dark apartment. His fist closed over her keys. He would give them back once he was inside.

"Would you like coffee, or something?" she asked, diffidently pausing.

"Yes." He stepped inside and closed the door behind him. Opening his palm, he offered her keys.

The brush of her fingertips against his skin strengthened the shimmering attraction that hovered all day. Without a word, he pulled her into his arms and kissed her.

She pushed against him after a moment and broke free. "I don't think we should be doing that," she said, her eyes lowered.

"Why not?" he asked. He'd kissed her before. She'd never protested.

Turning, almost running, Rennie headed for the kitchen. "I'll fix some coffee and we can talk for a bit. Then you'll have to leave. I have to get up early tomorrow—" She stopped suddenly as if she'd run out of words.

"Why do you have to get up early on a Sunday?" he asked, following her. What was wrong? She had changed in the few moments from the car to her apartment. He thought they had spent a pleasant day together. Suddenly it was as if she couldn't stand to be near him.

"I just do, all right? Do you want cream in your coffee?"

"No, I drink it black." He was disappointed she hadn't remembered. Which was stupid. Just because he remembered she liked hers laced liberally with cream didn't mean she had to pay attention to his likes or dislikes.

Leaning casually against the counter, his arms crossed over his chest, he watched her start the coffee machine, take cups down from the cupboard and rummage in the refrigerator for cream. She turned on the water, let it run hot, and dampened a dishrag, wiping the immaculate counters.

"Something bothering you, Rennie?" he asked. Tension stretched between them, rising every moment. There was definitely something wrong, but he couldn't figure out what it was.

"No. Coffee will be ready in a minute, why don't you go sit in the living room?"

"I don't mind waiting here," he said easily, his eyes never leaving her.

"I do, you make me nervous."

Marc raised his eyebrows in surprise to hear anything made her nervous. "I make you nervous?"

She nodded and swallowed hard, licking her lips and looking thoroughly exasperated. Instantly Marc wanted to feel that moisture on her lips with his, kiss her throat, feel that pulse point beat against his lips.

"You keep staring at me," she snapped, glaring at him.

He smiled and nodded. "You're easy on the eyes."

"Well, take your eyes and go in the living room. I'll bring the coffee out when it's done."

Marc shrugged and pushed away from the counter. Her behavior baffled him, but he had not come up with her to make her angry. If she wanted a few minutes to herself, he'd give it to her. He glanced out her window, but the swirling fog hid any view she might claim. Taking a seat on the comfortable sofa, he leaned back on the cushions, stretching his legs out. The room was fussy for his tastes, but reflected the romanticism that comprised much of Rennie's makeup. It was growing on him.

Five minutes later she joined him, a mug of coffee in each hand. Carefully placing them on the low table before the sofa, she chose the nearby chair, rather than join Marc on the sofa.

"You wanted to talk?" He didn't want to talk. He wanted her to sit beside him, where he could feel her presence, be enticed by her scent, touch her, kiss her.

"I thought I'd give you a thumbnail sketch of the women I think will be at the party next Saturday. You can decide ahead of time which ones you might like to meet so we don't miss anyone who would be a qualified candidate."

"I think I need to meet them all."

Rennie sighed and reached for her coffee cup. "The thing is, Marc, sometimes I don't think you are putting forth the effort you need in order to find a wife. I can only do so much. You should have taken Julie or Marcella out today. You are wasting time with me. I'm not your type."

"I enjoyed the day. And probably for the very reason that there is nothing between us except a business deal. Think how awkward it would be if you were interested in me from a romantic point."

"Right." She blew on her coffee and took a sip, her eyes on the cup. "Enjoy it while you can," she muttered. "The clock strikes midnight and it all ends."

"What do you mean?"

She glanced up, looked away. "Nothing much. Think about it for a minute. It was obvious today that you don't often spend your Saturdays as we did. And probably won't after you marry your paragon."

"You don't think my future wife can enjoy the kind of day we just spent?"

"I do have trouble picturing Marcella wanting to take a bay cruise in the fog. Or anytime, for that matter. And I doubt she'd ride a cable car unless every cab in the city was on strike."

"Marcella is out of the running, I told you that." He didn't like the trend of the conversation. Time enough later to talk about a future wife. He wanted to enjoy the rest of the evening with Rennie. Her perspective on things was refreshing, a bit wacky sometimes, but always kind and optimistic. He liked her enthusiasm for the ordinary, and her genuine interest in living for the moment.

"My point is, that if you want sophisticated and elegant, you are not going to get rowdy and adventuresome. The two don't mesh. Not that I would presume to tell you what kind of wife you need. You seem very certain of what you want."

"I am," he said firmly. He'd thought about it for years. He knew exactly the kind of woman he wanted for his wife, for the mother of his son. He had enough money to attract anyone he wanted. For a moment he looked at Rennie. She would be disappointed in his thoughts. She believed so much in love, and wanted it for everyone. "Your father and mother loved each other, I presume," he said.

"Passionately." She smiled, lost in memories for a moment. "I was too young then to really realize how special that love was. But they were forever kissing and touching and caressing each other, and me. Hugs were plentiful, kisses abundant. And I still remember the dazed disbelief with which my mother lived for years after he died. It was as if a part of herself was gone forever.''

"But she remarried.''

"About five years later. Theo had known her for a long time, but it was as if she couldn't see any man for years. Then she began to date again. Theo was number three, I think. And the last man she went out with. He wooed her in every way imaginable.''

"And had the money to afford extravagant gestures, I bet.''

Rennie flared up at that. "Take that back! It wasn't anything like that! He loves her and did everything he could to show her that, but he didn't need to spend a lot of money to do it. And Mom wouldn't have been impressed with money. She came from money. But she and Daddy didn't have much. The love they shared was so strong, they didn't miss having tons of money. Theo was smart enough to realize that and did not flaunt his wealth. If anything, it would have turned Mom off!''

Marc held out a hand, palm out. She looked like a kitten, ruffled fur and hissing. "Back off, wildcat. My mistake. I knew your mother refused to move home after your father died. My mistake thinking she'd like an easier life with Theo than struggling to make ends meet on her own.''

"Shows what you know, Mr. Rich Man.''

"Change of subject. I've engaged a limousine for Saturday. Where is this party? I need to let the driver know.''

"A limo? Why can't you drive? Or I can if you like. It's just to Toddy and Denise's. They live in Westborough. Jeez, Marc, we don't need a limo.''

"Indulge me, sweets. I might care to have a drink or two at the party and don't want to drink and drive."

"And you can afford it," she said waspishly.

"I prefer to look on it as putting a bit of money back into the economy."

Rennie laughed aloud. "I can't believe you said that. You no more think about putting money into the economy than...than you believe in love."

Since his diversion succeeded in drawing a response that was spontaneous and sincere, he decided to leave before she got herself worked up over something unimportant again.

"Thanks for the coffee. I'll pick you up next Saturday at seven-thirty."

She blinked. "You're leaving already. You haven't finished your coffee."

"It's time to go." He rose and waited for her to stand up.

"Thank you for a great day, Marc. I had fun."

"I did, too, Rennie." He walked to the door. Leaning over, he skimmed his lips over hers. He didn't hold her, or press his luck. She'd already rejected him once tonight, he didn't want a second time.

"Marc." She reached out and touched his arm. "Money is only important when you don't have it. You're not that poor kid living in the Tenderloin now. You have enough money that if you stopped work tomorrow, you would never want for anything again. There is more to life than just acquiring money and spending it. Let yourself discover the other joys out there."

"Philosophy at ten o'clock?" he asked dryly.

She nodded, her eyes serious and sincere. "Find your

perfect wife, but make sure you like her and can enjoy life with her. Marriage is for such a long time.''

"I know what I want, Rennie. And when I get it, I'll hold on to it.''

Twice during the week Marc almost called Rennie. Each time he hesitated. Her manner at her apartment disturbed him. She'd seemed different, remote almost. He knew he'd pushed for their date, but she had enjoyed herself, he knew it. She was too transparent to dissemble about that.

He wondered if she were seeing Joseph Thurmond Sanger. Would it be better to know one way or the other, or better to remain ignorant? He didn't want her dating Joe, but he had no hold over her. She was free to see whomever she wished.

Each time he reached for the phone, he changed his mind. He'd wait until Saturday.

Promptly at seven-thirty Marc rang the doorbell to Rennie's apartment. When she opened the door, he was stunned.

"Come in. I still have to get my shoes,'' she said, her eyes sparkling.

But the sparkle in her eyes barely outshone the sparkle in the diamonds that she wore. Marc stepped inside and stared at her. Twirling his index finger, he motioned her to turn around.

The dark blue dress appeared to have been designed solely for her. It fit like a second skin, displaying every taut curve, every sleek line. Ending above her knees, it displayed her shapely black nylon-clad legs to full advantage. The thin straps and low neckline perfectly framed the bib of diamonds that hung around her throat.

Diamond ear studs caught the light and drew the eye to the sleek hairstyle that looked as unlike Rennie as anything he'd just seen. Dramatic and sophisticated, it changed her entirely. The makeup emphasized her eyes, and the perfection of her lips. Sleek and sophisticated were excellent choices of words to describe the vision before him.

"Rennie?"

"What?" Those dramatic eyes narrowed as she stared at him.

"Just checking to make sure it was the right woman. You look fantastic."

She grinned, and he recognized the lopsided smile. "I clean up real good, wouldn't you say? Have to hold my own at these kinds of events. I'll see everyone in my age group at this party. And most of them use any excuse to try for one-upmanship. I've often thought a really smart thief would hit up one of these and take all the jewelry we're wearing. He could retire for life after such a heist."

"Get your shoes. The limo is waiting."

He watched her hurry to her bedroom, entranced with the sway of her hips, the sassy flash of legs as she moved soundlessly down the hall. For a moment he hesitated, unsure he wanted to go to the party. He'd rather stay home and discover more about Rennie. The last thing he'd expected tonight was to find her dressed like a fashion model and carrying off the sophistication he'd glimpsed in Suzanne and Marcella.

Yet why not? She'd grown up with Suzanne, Marcella and Julie. She'd gone to the right schools, came from old money and had a mother who probably taught her everything she needed to know to hold her own in San Francisco society.

How many other facets were there to this woman?

When she left her bedroom, she wore strappy high heels and carried an evening wrap. Detouring through the living room, she scooped up a fancy wrapped present, and hurried to join Marc.

"Should I have bought a gift?" he asked, spying the package she carried.

"Nope. You don't even know them yet. But I've been friends with Denise for years."

"Didn't you say you hadn't planned to attend, until you decided it would be the perfect place for me to meet your friends?"

She nodded.

He indicated the dress and diamonds. "Last-minute choice? No worrying about nothing to wear?"

"Yes, well it is a bit much, sometimes." She ran her hand down over her hips, and Marc followed, wishing it was his hand following the soft flare of hip. "This is not really me. I prefer wearing jeans like last weekend. And there will be so many people there, I won't really get to visit much with Toddy and Denise, so it seemed like a waste of time. But now we have another goal."

"Toddy, is that a nickname?" Marc reached out to draw her wrap from her arms and hold it for her to put on.

"His actual name is William. But in college he fell prey to hot toddies. He loved them, and usually ended up drunk as a skunk. So the nickname stuck. He doesn't imbibe quite so freely now that he's gained a bit of wisdom. But if you ever want to bribe him, do it with a hot toddy."

"I doubt I need to bribe anyone," Marc murmured, drawing in a deep breath. The soft fragrance that was pure Rennie delighted him. He'd missed it this past week. He'd missed her.

"Well, let's get this show on the road. And, Marc..." She caught his arm and looked into his eyes. "This is it. You will find someone tonight, or all bets are off. And I have fulfilled my part of this crazy deal you and Keith concocted. You have to go into this with an open mind. Do you hear?"

He smiled, amused by her lecture. "I hear. I'll let you know later if the deal has been fulfilled."

Anger flashed in her eyes, but he didn't care. Leaning closer he kissed her. The taste of lip gloss different from that of her natural lips. Beneath it, he could feel her warmth.

"We'll talk later," he promised. "Come, my lady, your coach awaits. Did I tell you how beautiful you look tonight?"

She shook her head and slowly allowed a small smile. "Sleek and sophisticated?" she asked slyly.

"Definitely. Maybe I should be looking a bit closer to home for a bride?"

Her smile saddened. "No, Marc. We wouldn't suit. The things we each want are too different."

She was right, of course. But for a moment he let the fantasy invade his mind. Marrying Rennie, living with her in his apartment overlooking the marina. They'd each go to work in the morning, meet for lunch a couple of times a week, cook dinner together. And the weekends, the ones he didn't spend at the boys' club, would be spent together, doing things together. He wouldn't be alone anymore. He wouldn't be consumed with work. He'd have Rennie.

Lights blazed from every window in the house the limo stopped before. The sound of laughter, conversation and soft music wafted from the windows, left open to cool down the rooms. The driver opened the back door and Marc assisted Rennie from the vehicle, glad he'd hired the limo. There wasn't a parking place in sight.

Rennie handed the gift and her wrap to the maid who opened the door. Glancing at Marc, her eyes widened.

"Oops." She brushed his lips with her thumb, then a second time.

"Lipstick," she muttered, looking at the red stain on her thumb.

He chuckled and drew out his handkerchief. Running it over his mouth once to make sure she'd gotten all traces, he took her hand and began to wipe the smear from her thumb.

"Hazards of kissing a beautiful woman dressed to the nines," he murmured.

"Do I need to replenish it?" she asked, tilting her head up for his perusal.

"Not unless I kiss you again."

She backed away. "Not here."

"I'm not exactly an ogre." Anger touched him at her retreat.

"Of course not, you idiot. But you're here looking for someone else. If people see you kissing me they are going to get entirely the wrong impression."

"I'm not sure I give a damn."

"Rennie, how nice to see you." A tall red-haired woman sailed into the foyer. "I thought I heard the bell a minute ago. How have you been?" She touched her cheek to Rennie's and smiled in welcome.

"Hi, Denise. I've been great. You look wonderful. Happy anniversary. Marriage obviously agrees with you."

"Oh, honey, it's more than that. Toddy and I are expecting!"

"Wow! I can't believe it. You two are going to be parents?"

"Yes, but not for about seven more months. In the meantime, I don't believe I know your date." Denise linked arms with Rennie and smiled brightly at Marc.

"Oh, sorry. Marc, I'd like you to meet Denise. Denise, this is Marc Foster."

"How nice to meet you, Marc. I've heard a lot about you, mostly from the papers. Keith is here and he said he thought you'd be coming with Rennie. Come on in and mingle. We've got to get together soon, Rennie."

"Absolutely, Denise. I want to hear all about the blessed event."

The large living room was crowded with men and women talking, laughing and moving from group to group. Few people used the furniture, most were standing. Rennie hesitated in the archway.

"Do you want to get a drink or something before we begin to mingle?" she asked Marc.

"Fine."

She led the way to the dining room where the long table had been pushed to one wall and was ladened with canapés. By the door to the kitchen a bar had been set up. They ordered drinks from the bartender.

"Hi, Rennie. I didn't know you were coming." A tall, thin young man bent to kiss her cheek. She smiled at him.

"Hi, Joe. I didn't plan to come originally, but then decided I needed to toast the happy couple."

When the man looked at Marc, Rennie rushed into speech.

"Marc, this is Joe. Joe, Marc."

Joe nodded his head once. "Marc."

Suspecting who the man was, Marc stepped closer to Rennie and placed his hand on her shoulder. Her bare shoulder. Slipping his fingers beneath the thin straps that held her dress, he pulled her closer. "Joe as in Joseph Thurmond Sanger the Fourth?" he asked, his narrowed gaze assessing the man before him.

In other circumstances, he might have liked him. Joe carried himself confidently without an arrogant swagger. Apparently completely at ease in the surroundings. Of course, he'd been born to this life. Marc resented him instantly.

Joe laughed and looked at Rennie, his eyes lingering on the possessive hold Marc had made.

"You didn't tell him that, did you?" he asked Rennie.

Color rose in her cheeks and she looked confused. "I think I did ages ago. Why not, it's your name."

"Come on, Rennie—Joseph Thurmond Sanger the Fourth? I don't go around telling friends you are Renata Elizabeth Morgan the First."

Before she could reply, Marc tightened his grip. Joe knew her middle name, he hadn't. He didn't like the implied intimacy between the two.

"Excuse us, Joe? Rennie's promised to introduce me to someone."

"Sure. Nice to meet you."

Marc couldn't parrot the words. He nodded and moved from the large room, dodging another couple, sheltering Rennie from bumping into them.

"I can't believe that." She took a sip of her drink and stopped dead. "I just can't believe you did that. Get your hand off me."

"Don't cause a scene," he said, moving his hand, reluctant to release that tantalizing soft skin.

"Don't cause a scene? You haven't seen anything if you think my calmly asking you to remove your hand is a scene. But if you want one, I'm just the person to cause it."

"I don't want one. What's wrong? I just put my hand on your shoulder."

"Listen, I've been around men long enough to recognize a possessive move. You almost stood on a table and told Joe hands off. I can't believe you did that." She looked at him suspiciously. "You acted almost jealous," she accused.

"In case you forgot, we are here tonight for you to introduce me to eligible candidates for my wife, not to meet all your boyfriends."

"All my— One man! And he's not a boyfriend. He's just a friend."

"Marc? This is getting to be a habit, man." Keith stopped and held out his hand. "Whoa, did you bring Rennie?" he asked as the men shook hands.

"She brought me," Marc replied.

"Much to my regret, I might add," she said, seething. "You're here now, Keith, you take him under control. I have to go to the ladies."

Marc reached out and caught her arm. "Truly?"

"Truly," she said sweetly. "Otherwise I'm tempted to throw this glass of wine over your head!"

She pulled away and stormed across the room.

"Trouble in paradise?" Keith asked, watching his cousin.

"Nothing I can't handle," Marc replied. He watched as she rounded a corner and was lost from sight.

"Right. You can handle anything. So how do you like Rennie?"

"She's enough to drive a man crazy."

"Yes. But isn't she a love?"

Marc closed his eyes briefly at the word. Opening them, he looked at Keith.

"She brought me tonight to meet some of her friends."

"I thought you two were a duo," Keith said, puzzled.

"I can't imagine why. She's not what I'm looking for in a wife," Marc replied blandly.

Bridling, Keith's gaze hardened. "Why not?"

"Back off, Keith. Rennie and I just wouldn't suit. I'm looking for a bit more sophistication—"

"Did you see her tonight? She's as sophisticated as they get."

"She's looking for love, and I don't even believe in it," Marc said.

"Not believe in it, or just never experienced it?" Keith asked shrewdly.

"Neither. My parents said they loved each other, and look at the hell they made of their lives. My father said he loved me, and neglected me, did not provide for me, did not care for anyone or anything but liquor. Love is an illusion, and one I plan to do without."

"I loved Betsy. I still miss her, every day."

"She died twelve years ago, Keith, get over it. Get on with life."

"Right. I could be a workaholic like you. Rennie's a saint to put up with you. I'm sorry now that I suggested the plan. I hope you find someone tonight so she's out of it."

Keith spun around and headed for the bar. He never looked back.

"Damn," Marc said softly.

"Marc?" Marcella Randolph stopped and smiled at

him. "Nice to see you again. I didn't know you were a friend of Toddy's."

"I came with Rennie. In fact I have yet to meet the host, though Denise greeted us at the door," he said, already wishing Rennie had returned.

"Come on and I'll introduce you around. Where did Rennie go?"

By the time Marc spotted Rennie sometime later, he'd met four young women, friends of Marcella's. Studying them casually, he found himself completely unmoved by any of them. Keeping an eye open for Rennie, his mind had wandered. He knew she was mad at his behavior when meeting her friend Joe, but dammit, she had made a bargain, and he expected her to be making the introductions, and giving him background information on the people he met, not Marcella. Where was she?

Spying her near the door, Marc left the group he'd been a part of and headed in Rennie's direction. She'd had enough time to sulk.

"Rennie, are you all right?" he asked when he drew close enough.

She nodded. "Fine." Taking a breath, she tossed her head and smiled. It didn't reach her eyes. "Let's mingle, Marc. That's our sole reason for being here, right?"

"Marcella's introduced me to a few people." He didn't want to meet any more women. What he'd really like to do was take Rennie to the Crown Room and dance away the rest of the night. She looked so polished and lovely, he wanted to show her off to the world at the same time keep her for himself. Just the two of them.

"Who did you meet?"

"Christine Williams and her current date. Joyce Montgomery. Ellen Naylor."

"Ellen would be a good choice. Did you like her?"

He shrugged. "She didn't brag about her father's wealth or talk my ear off."

"Good start. Let's go find her and spend a bit more time with her." Rennie led the way purposefully.

So much for his idea of dancing.

By the end of the evening Marc's temper was frayed. He knew a wrong word would unleash his anger. Rennie had been the perfect matchmaker, drawing out Ellen and pointing out how much in common she and Marc had. At just the right moment, she'd excused herself and left the two of them near one of the windows. Marc easily drew the young woman out further, but one part of him centered on Rennie. He watched as she mingled with friends, kissed some, hugged some. Jealousy rose again. He wanted her attention on him. Wanted those kisses and hugs.

A discreet glance at his watch showed him it was almost time for the limo to arrive. Grateful he'd indicated a time to the driver, he explained to Ellen that he had to leave. Fully aware she met many of the attributes he claimed he wanted in a wife, he asked if he could call her. She smiled and nodded, seeming pleased as she recited her phone number.

When he finished jotting it down, Marc's gaze clashed with Rennie's. For a moment he couldn't read her expression, but just before she turned away, it looked shocked. And sad.

CHAPTER EIGHT

MARC sensed the tension in Rennie as they waited for the limousine. It swirled around them as the car drew up and they entered the luxury vehicle. When the door closed, enclosing them in the wide breadth of the car, Marc turned to her.

"Is there a problem?" he asked, on the alert. He knew something was wrong, but he was unable to pinpoint exactly what.

"Should there be? It seems as if we accomplished exactly what you wanted this evening. I introduced you to several eligible women whose families don't have a skeleton in the closet, or a hidden agenda. You seemed especially chummy with Ellen Naylor. Is she the one, do you think? I'm sure she would be a malleable wife. Just what you need to display the family jewels." Her voice sounded distant, uninterested.

"Far too early to tell. I have her phone number. I thought I'd give her a call and invite her to dinner. I don't wish to chance lunch." He hoped for a smile at that, but Rennie's lips were clamped in a distinctive line of disapproval.

After a moment she nodded. "Sounds like a good plan."

"Any thoughts on how I should handle this?" Marc asked a few moments later when Rennie remained silent.

She looked at him. "I'm sure you can manage just fine. Be yourself, spend lots of money on her and she'll love you to death. Oh, no, not love. Well, she'll be glad to spend time with you. Help you decide how to spend all that money. You could have asked her when you two were being so chummy.''

''We had other things to discuss.'' Could it be she resented the time he spent with Ellen? Was Rennie jealous? What else could account for her cold voice, her snippy manner?

''I'm sure you did. And did she pass muster? Must have if you have invited her out. She's already ahead of Marcella and Julie.''

''On the surface she seems to meet my requirements,'' he said calmly, intrigued by her behavior. Not for the first time he wished he understood women better.

Rennie shook her head. ''Still sounds like you're getting a dog.''

''I find her charming and likable. And she is easy on the eyes. Tell me some more about Ellen,'' he invited, interested to see if she thawed at all, or stayed cool. Was she jealous of his attention to Ellen? Did she want his attention focused on herself?

The car slid silently through the dark city streets, the motion soothing, in direct contrast to the tension that filled the interior. There was something wrong, but he couldn't pinpoint exactly what it was. Had someone said something to upset Rennie, or was it more personal? For a moment he almost yielded to the urge to demand she tell him what the problem was so he could fix it.

''Ellen's family has been in California for generations. Her father inherited a lot of money, and made even more in shipping. He branched into computers when Apple first started, and increased the family wealth drastically. And they take care of their wealth. You'll have no worries about her marrying you for your money. She has more than she can spend in a lifetime. But I don't think she brags on her family's wealth like Marcella,'' Rennie said.

''And should I worry about any other aspect with Ellen?'' he asked quickly.

She looked at him in confusion. ''I can't imagine what. She's been to the best schools, excels in small talk and probably will be totally intrigued with you. You've amassed a fortune, run a tremendously successful company, are welcomed everywhere, you two seem the perfect match with entrée everywhere.''

''Like your family welcomed me,'' he said softly.

''You're Keith's friend. I know Aunt Patty is fond of you as is Uncle Keith. Why wouldn't they welcome you? You're a bit dictatorial, but kind and generous with your time, look at your volunteer work. I don't know many men who give so much of themselves. Most just send money.''

He shrugged.

''Anyway, I'm sure Ellen will be beside herself to be going out with you,'' she muttered, scooting farther away on the plush seat and staring out the tinted windows as the lights flashed by. ''At least our deal is complete.''

''Not yet.''

''Why not? I've fulfilled my part. I introduced you to half a dozen eligible women tonight. You liked Ellen, you said you're going to invite her out. What more do you want?''

''Some pointers on what she'd like, maybe.'' He was clutching at straws, it sounded silly. But he didn't like Rennie's mentioning that their deal was ended. He wasn't ready to stop seeing Rennie.

''Take her to some fancy-do restaurant, order

champagne, dance until the place closes. She'll love that. Make it very romantic. Women love that.''

"Do you?''

"Do I what?'' Rennie looked at him warily.

"Like things romantic.''

"We aren't discussing me. We're trying to finish this dumb deal. You like Ellen. Marry her and we're quits.''

"Not quite. It's a bit early yet. Ellen and I may not suit.''

"For God's sake, Marc, am I suppose to dangle until you finally tie the knot? Our agreement was to introduce you to eligible women. I've done it.''

"It is finished when I say so. Since I hold the high cards, you don't have much to say in the matter.''

She frowned and edged further away. If she moved any more, he thought, she'd be up against the door.

As the limo turned onto Chestnut Street, Marc realized if he called Ellen and liked her, he might well be on his way to marrying into an old San Francisco family. The exultation he expected was missing. Too early to feel triumph at achieving his goal. Time enough for that if he decided Ellen was the one. Glancing at Rennie, he realized if he and Ellen clicked that he would see Rennie occasionally as friends of both he and his wife. Somehow the thought disturbed.

"Do you need me to come to the boutique to help with your accounting?'' he asked, wanting another tie to connect them. He wasn't ready to give up his tentative friendship with this woman, not yet.

"I can manage. Just send the canceled note.'' She waited in silence as the driver hurried to open her door.

"I'll call you after Ellen and I meet, in case I need further pointers.'' He opened the back door and stepped to the curb, reaching out to assist Rennie.

"No need. Just send the canceled note. And I can get up to my apartment by myself." She turned and almost ran up the three stone steps to the heavy front door.

Marc ignored her snappish behavior and accompanied her to her apartment. Reaching calmly for her keys, he was startled at how cold her fingers felt.

"Are you all right?" he asked.

"Fine. Goodbye, Marc." She snatched the keys from his fingers and hurried inside, closing the door in his face.

"Good night," he said, anger beginning to build. He wasn't used to temperamental prima donnas. If that was how creative people reacted, he would do better to stick with businessmen.

"The hell with it," Marc swore Sunday afternoon. All morning he'd been tempted to call Rennie to see if she wanted to spend the afternoon together. He'd spent the previous day at the boys' club working with the youngsters. The satisfaction he derived from sharing his time with those boys quietly filled a needed space within.

But the party they'd attended last night had fulfilled nothing. He didn't often attend such functions, but in an effort to find the right mate, he'd gone. And if Ellen turned out to be someone he could seriously consider, the event would be well worth it.

Now Sunday was passing with agonizing slowness. He had enjoyed last Saturday with Rennie. He wondered if she'd be interested in wandering around the wharf again, or maybe taking a hike in Golden Gate Park.

Dialing her number, the anticipation that built surprised him. He had just seen her last night, and their parting had been less than satisfactory. Her attitude at the end of the evening should have put him off women.

Contrary creatures. Instead, he wanted to talk to her, hear her prattle on about the party, or a dress she was designing or the newest wedding she had promised to choreograph. He could ask her more questions about Ellen, find out more about the woman who might one day be his wife.

The phone rang endlessly.

Reluctantly Marc hung up. She wasn't home. Out with Joe? The thought burned. Damn, he had no right to be jealous of her time when not with him. She was merely helping him out in exchange for relief on the loan from his company. If he didn't have that hold over her, would she spend any time with him? Would she willingly help him find the kind of wife he wanted? He sheered away from guessing the answer, knowing he probably would not like it.

Marc wandered around his living room, crossing to the window to stare out at the clear sky. There were things he could do. Accounts at the office that he could study. His mind went blank. There was nothing else. For the first time in years he had nothing he wanted to do, except talk to Rennie. The attraction of work paled. He had few outside interests, few friends. Goal-oriented since his childhood, he'd set a target and pushed forward until he achieved it. But leisure time had not been important. He had no hobbies, no burning interests aside from work.

And now his goal of marriage and a son.

Or daughter, as Rennie had suggested. For a moment a smile touched his lips. He could envision a bundle of energy with blond hair and bright blue eyes running up to him to share something, a new dolly, or a picture she'd drawn. He'd study it gravely and announce that it was perfect. As that precious little girl would be.

Turning away in disgust, he frowned. He wasn't planning to make a baby with Rennie. She didn't fit his vision of the perfect wife.

The image of Rennie as she'd been last night rose. Sleek, sophisticated, polished. She held her own with every other woman there. Even her normal exuberance had been dampened, until she personified his ideal woman, his image for a wife.

But it was false. That wasn't the real Rennie. The woman he was coming to know was casual and spontaneous, embracing everything life had to offer with wild abandon. Kicking off her shoes whenever possible, she did not pretend to be sophisticated and blasé about life. Instead, she sallied forth with enthusiasm and childlike delight. And for a few hours, whenever in her company, she opened the world to him in a way he'd never seen before.

She was different, that was it. A novelty. He'd grow tired of it after a while. She expected more from him than he wanted to give. His world was ordered, just the way he wanted it. He'd worked hard to achieve all he had, now it was time to move to the next stage, a marriage alliance that would cement his achievements and assure his acceptance in the society of the city.

But he wasn't married yet, and if he wanted to spend more time with Rennie Morgan, he'd damn well do so. He pulled the portable phone from the stand and punched in her number. He hadn't achieved all he had by giving up easily. And he didn't plan to give up on reaching Rennie today, either.

By nine that night, Marc finally admitted defeat. He'd tried calling her every fifteen minutes throughout the afternoon and evening. Obviously she'd gone out and he didn't know when she'd be home.

For all he knew she planned to spend the night away from home. And if so, who with? Jealousy simmered just below the surface. And anger. And a bit of frustration that she didn't care to spend her afternoon with him. He knew she'd enjoyed last weekend, that was one thing he liked about her, she didn't dissemble. She let people know instantly if she liked or disliked something.

Monday morning Marc called the boutique. Eve answered the phone.

"Rennie, please," Marc said, settling back, anticipating her voice.

"Sorry, she's busy right now. May I take a message?"

"This is Marc Foster."

"Can I help you? Or take a message for Rennie?"

Did her voice sound cautious? Used to reading people when making deals involving vast amounts of money, he paid strict attention.

"When she's free, have her call me."

"Um, that might be quite a while. Is there anything I can do?"

"I'll wait for her call." Marc wasn't going to be fobbed off with Rennie's assistant. He wanted Rennie.

He hung up. Damn, what was with the woman?

Ten minutes later Rachel put through a call from Eve.

"Mr. Foster, Rennie asked me to let you know she's going to be tied up most of the day and asked if I'd call you. If there is anything urgent, maybe I could help?"

"Doing what?"

"I beg your pardon?"

"What is Rennie doing all day that she can't take five minutes to return a call?"

"Um, we have a full schedule today. If there is anything I can do, please let me know. Rennie said to tell you good luck with Ellen." Eve said a polite goodbye.

Marc swore softly. Staring at the phone he wondered if he even wanted to call Ellen. She'd seemed the perfect candidate on Saturday night, but he was more interested in Rennie at the moment. From her odd attitude Saturday, to being away from home all day yesterday, to this latest development. What was going on?

He hit redial and waited. Eve answered again.

"Tell Rennie I want to speak to her this morning. If I don't hear from her, the deal changes. All bets off. Tell her that." He hung up before Eve could say a word.

It took longer than he had expected to get the call. Rachel buzzed him just prior to lunch.

"Rennie Morgan on line two," she said efficiently.

Glancing at his watch, he saw it was almost noon. "Cutting it a bit close, aren't you?" he said when he made the connection.

"I'm busy. What do you want?" Anger shimmered across the lines.

"I wanted to talk to you."

"So just because you want to talk, my life has to go on hold? I'm supposed to drop everything? Who do you think you are?"

"The man who holds the note on your business," Marc replied coolly.

The silence fairly seethed.

"Are you free for lunch?" he asked.

"No."

Marc waited, surprised that a torrent of words wasn't forthcoming. Rennie usually talked forever.

"Rennie—"

"Look, Marc. I am busy. I don't have time to stop and pander to your whim for lunch. Call Ellen. You have her number. I have to go. Do what you want about the note." The phone slammed down.

Serve her right if he called the note today.

But he wouldn't. He preferred to have Rennie owe him. That way he'd have a reason to see her again.

He flicked the paper with Ellen's phone number on it. He'd hold off another day before calling her.

Marc rang the doorbell. Dressed in jeans and a pullover shirt, he hoped he was casual enough to suit his snippy friend. He glanced at the leather running shoes. Probably too formal. Maybe he should try the bare-footed look.

Rennie opened the door, surprise clearly evident on her face. Was there also a trace of joy? He couldn't be sure. Instantly she masked her expression, blanking all emotion from her face.

"I wasn't expecting you," she said.

He smiled. Always catch the opposition off guard had been a maxim of his for years. "May I come in?" He raised the flowers and handed them to her.

The smile that lit her eyes couldn't be blanked out, he thought gratefully.

"They're lovely," she murmured as she slowly reached for the bouquet.

Relief was almost tangible. He'd taken a risk buying daisies and carnations rather than roses. But he wasn't here for hearts and flowers, he'd come to visit a friend. Every woman loved flowers, and when he'd passed the vendor on the corner, he had not resisted. Rennie's smile was worth the unusual impulse.

"I guess you're staying?" she asked, looking over the colorful display.

He nodded.

"Have a seat, I'll put them in water."

If he didn't know better, he'd think she was flustered. Ignoring her invitation, he followed her into the kitchen.

He leaned against the doorjamb, watching her hunt for a large vase.

"Why are you here?" she asked when she found one in the far back corner of a cupboard. Running water in it, she kept her eyes carefully averted from Marc.

"Wanted to see you," he said easily.

"Why?"

"Beats me. You've been in a bad mood for days."

She shrugged, arranging the flowers in the vase to suit her, a slow smile tugging at her lips. Marc wanted to feel that smile against his own mouth, wanted to gather her up and kiss her until they both had trouble breathing. He wanted to feel her feminine body pressed tightly against his, taste her sweetness, savor the fragrance that surrounded her. Capture some of the heat and excitement and very essence of Rennie Morgan.

He folded his arms across his chest and took a breath. Not yet. Maybe later, but first he was going to get to the bottom of her weird behavior.

"Business is brisk apparently," he murmured.

"Yes." She fussed with the flowers until he wanted to take the bunch and toss them in the sink. Maybe they had not been such a good idea. He wanted her to look at him, not the damn blossoms.

"Did you get your accounts in order?"

Rennie looked over the flowers as she turned, holding the vase as if a shield. "Is that why you came tonight? To check up on my books?"

"No."

She walked toward him, her expression wary.

Marc debated remaining exactly as he was. He wondered if she'd push against him to move him, or stop and keep her distance. Curious, he nevertheless moved aside and let her pass. Her distinctive fragrance filled the air. His fingers clenched into a tight fist to keep from reaching out to thread through her soft hair, to touch that velvet skin.

"So why did you come tonight?" she asked as she settled the vase on the table in the living room. Soft music played in her stereo, a book had been laid face-down on the floor beside her chair.

"To see you."

"Did you call Ellen?" she asked, standing before the window. There was little that welcomed him about her stance. She was rigid and wary.

"Not yet." He sat on her sofa and stared at her. "Are you going to stand there all night?"

Shaking her head, she moved to sit on the chair, tucking her feet beneath her. Tonight they were covered in bright yellow socks. There were no shoes in evidence.

"Why haven't you called Ellen?"

"No rush, is there?"

"I thought you were in a rush. I thought you wanted to get settled before your next birthday, or something."

Did he imagine an almost imperceptible thawing?

"It would be nice, but not earth-shattering if I don't make it. Some things take time."

"Ellen's nice."

"So you say. Tell me about how busy you've been this week."

She fidgeted with the edge of her shirt. "Lots of people are planning weddings in the next few months. I've been recommended by several former clients who had very successful ones. Things are picking up." She glanced up suddenly. "If you don't foreclose soon, I think I'll be able to make a big payment on the loan. If you are worried about losing money on the deal, you can rest assured that you won't."

He nodded gravely. "Thank you, I'll sleep better knowing that."

She frowned, then laughed softly. "As if the few thousand lousy bucks your company lent me are more than a drop in your bucket. I can't imagine you losing sleep over something like that. In fact, I bet you sleep fine every night."

"Mostly." He settled back, stretching his legs out, tucking his hands behind the waistband of his jeans. Resting his head on the back of her sofa, he half closed his eyes and watched her. A deep feeling of contentment slowly permeated.

"Made up any new expensive dresses that people aren't buying?" he asked lazily.

She shook her head. "That dress is gorgeous. It'll sell someday. And I've taken your wise words to heart— now I ask for a deposit and will have the complete dress paid for before the final fitting. See what a good student I've proved to be?"

"Until someone comes along who can't afford something, and your soft heart gives away the store."

"You're so cynical. A wedding is a special time for a woman. Romantic and precious. I hate to intrude with the crassness of money."

"Yet if you don't, you won't be able to make their wedding dreams come true because you'll be out of business."

"Logical as well as cynical. Do you practice that, or did it come naturally? Joe is the same way, about some things."

"I don't want to talk about Joe," Marc said firmly.

She smiled, amusement dancing in her eyes. "Jealous?"

"Do you want me to be?"

Laughing gently, Rennie shook her head. "I guess not. And there's no reason to be, even if you were interested in me, which of course you are not. You want someone like Ellen. Right? Or Marcella if she didn't brag about money. Or maybe Julie if she could just be coerced into a bit more modesty about her volunteer work."

"Or maybe I haven't met the right woman yet."

She blinked. "Really? What other requirements do you want? I thought we went through everything."

"Do you think Ellen would be most suitable?"

Rennie hesitated a moment, her gaze dropping to her hand where she fiddled with the shirt hem again. "I suppose."

"But she wasn't one of the ones you invited to lunch."

"She's a bit quiet. I thought you needed someone a bit more lively. Marcella loves to entertain and Julie is quite polished that way. Ellen is more of a homebody. Which would be fine for you, I guess. Didn't you say you wanted your wife to stay home with your children?"

"Yes."

"That would be nice. I mean a lot of women would love to do that. Of course, you have to realize some of that comes from your own mother being gone when you were a child. If a woman isn't happy staying at home, doing so won't make it a good experience for the children. Lots of women work now, you know, and still raise healthy well-adjusted children. And you'll have a very strong, positive influence in your kids' lives."

"I plan to spend a lot of time with them."

"Just don't push them to do everything you wished you could have done as a child. I see that a lot, especially in wedding planning. The mother of the bride always wished for more than what she had as a bride and tries to get it through her daughter. A wedding should be so very personal with the bride, not a manifestation of her mother's dreams.''

"I don't plan to try to relive my childhood through my children."

"Good."

He watched her, knowing she couldn't keep still, or silent, for long.

"You look awfully relaxed," she said a moment later.

"I feel relaxed. You're easy to be with."

"Maybe you should practice being relaxed with Ellen." She frowned.

"Maybe Ellen isn't the right one."

Rennie sighed. "Honestly, Marc, you have to make some sort of effort with this project. I can't do everything."

"Some projects take time."

"Why did you come here tonight?"

"I wanted to see you."

"Oh." She shifted in the chair, glanced at him, glanced away.

Marc's amusement grew as her uncertainty and squirming increased.

"Did you want to talk about anything in particular?" she asked.

"No. Do you?"

"I could tell you about work. Or you could tell me about your work. Or we could talk about other women who might be suitable candidates for your wife."

"Or we could talk about something else. Is my finding a wife all that is between us?"

"What else could there be?"

"Friendship?" he suggested.

"For how long?"

"How long do you keep friends? Keith and I have been friends for seventeen years. I expect we'll stay friends for life."

"You want us to be friends for life?"

"Would that be a problem?" Suddenly he wanted her to commit to being his friend for life. He wanted to know he could count on her throughout the years, no matter who he married, no matter what happened with her shop. He wanted some certainty for the future. Would she give it?

"I don't know," she hedged.

"Come and sit beside me, Rennie." Marc patted the cushion beside him.

Every part of her appeared to go on alert. She became still, her eyes widened. "Why?"

Smiling slowly, he patted the sofa. His immediate urge was to yank her from that chair and into his arms, but he would pursue her slowly, cautiously. But he wanted her tonight and he always got what he wanted. Rennie was a babe in arms when compared to him.

She studied him and Marc wished he had access to her thoughts. He could almost see the vacillation, the arguments for and against moving. Finally, she huffed a short sigh and rose, crossing the room to sit beside him, watching him as warily as a rabbit would watch a wolf.

He reached his hand out and caught her, entwining their fingers. Leaning back again, he closed his eyes. Better to lure her into a feeling of safety before he moved to the next step. "Tell me about the weddings you planned this week."

When given a topic near and dear to her heart, Rennie could go on forever. Slowly, at first, she offered tidbits of her workday, growing in enthusiasm and excitement as he nodded in understanding as she explained the various aspects of complex wedding plans, from scheduling sought-after churches and dealing with fussy caterers, to the intricacies of accessories for the bride and her attendants.

Marc listened to her voice, enjoying the rich melodious tones as she expounded on her work. A man could do a lot worse than come home to someone like Rennie each day.

Startled at the trend of his thoughts, he opened his eyes and looked at her. Silky blond hair swirled around her face, a hint of pink tinged her cheeks, her blue eyes sparkled and shone. He tugged and she leaned closer, her sentence trailing off as her gaze locked with his, as she read the intent and desire he knew must be blazing in his eyes.

CHAPTER NINE

SHE stopped talking. He could see her swallow hard, her eyes questioning. Slowly he pulled her even closer, releasing her hand to encircle her. He wanted her in his embrace. He wanted to touch her, had shown outstanding restraint to wait this long. One hand cupped her chin. He traced his thumb along her jaw, brushing across her pink lips. They opened slightly and his heart kicked into high gear.

Lowering his face, he kissed her.

There was no response. Pulling back a fraction, he gazed down into her confused eyes.

"Rennie?" Smoothing the soft skin over her cheek, he watched the expressions chase around her face.

"I don't think this is such a good idea, Marc," she said softly.

"Why not?"

"I thought you were interested in Ellen."

"I enjoyed meeting her. Maybe I'll call her and see if she'd like to go out. But tonight I came to see you."

"Why?"

"Why not, aren't we friends?" He brushed his lips across hers once. Twice. She was so soft, so delightfully feminine. He wanted—

"I don't think we're friends." She leaned against his hands, but he didn't release her. "I thought we were business associates."

"And friends." He threaded his fingers in the silkiness of her hair and tilted her head slightly for better access. When he covered her mouth with his this time, she gave a soft sigh and responded. Her lips met his with a will all their own. When he moved to deepen the kiss, she opened her mouth and he tasted the honey sweetness.

He slipped his arm around her, drawing her up against his chest, reveling in the differences between their bodies, reveling in the feelings that surged through him when she pressed against him. He kissed her until they both longed for breath. Breaking apart, he smoothed her hair, brushed the fire in her cheeks. Her lips were rosy and slightly swollen. "That's nice."

She shoved against his chest and pushed herself to her feet. "Maybe too nice. You need to leave, Marc. This roller-coaster ride is too much for me. I fulfilled my part of the bargain. You need to remember your goal. It isn't to kiss up some *friend,* it's to get yourself your perfect wife, remember?"

"And does one preclude the other?" he asked lazily. His manner was deceptive. Every cell in his body raged to hold her again, to kiss her, make her his. But he had not succeeded in the cutthroat business of investing by showing the opposition his every thought. What was Rennie's problem?

"What about me?" she asked.

"What about you?" He stood and crossed the room to stand beside her. He fisted his hands, resisting the strong urge to gather her up again and resume their kiss.

"Maybe I don't want to be a substitute."

"A substitute? What are you talking about? I don't see you as some sort of substitute—for what?"

"You should be out romancing the woman you plan to marry, not kissing me." She turned away, dragging her fingers through her hair. "I'm busy, Marc, and not up to games right now. Take your killer kisses and give them to your trophy bride.''

''Killer kisses, huh?'' He reached for her shoulders, planning to turn her back to face him, but the tension that hummed through her body startled him. Slowly he massaged the tight muscles, lowering his head to rest beside hers. Softly he spoke. ''I like the sound of killer kisses, want to share some more?''

''No! I want you to leave!''

He spun her around at the note in her voice, shocked to see tears shimmering in her eyes.

''Rennie, what's wrong?''

''This is all wrong, that's what. I should not be trying to find you a wife, you should find your own. And you shouldn't settle for less than what everyone deserves, love and caring. Buying yourself some sophisticated woman to complement your lifestyle is just plain dumb. And I'm not going to be a part of it. I can't. I wish this had never started. I was much happier before.'' She sniffed, and brushed her eyes with her fingertips, but the tears spilled over and ran down her cheeks.

Marc felt a touch of panic. He hadn't a clue how to handle a crying woman. He remembered his mother crying once, and how helpless he felt as a child. The same feeling swamped him.

''Don't cry, Rennie.'' He hugged her, holding her as she struggled for control.

''I'll be fine. I'm tired, that's all. Just leave, please?'' She wiped her cheeks again and tried a smile.

It didn't make it, but he gave her credit for the effort. But the entreaty in her eyes reached him.

''I'll call you.''

''Don't. Marc, take Ellen out if you like, but give her a real chance. She's a person who wants to be loved as much as anyone. Don't shortchange her or yourself by denying the possibility. And if she's not the one you want, wait until you find the right one.''

"Love is fine for some romantic woman like you, wrapping yourself up in weddings and brides and lace and satin. But it's been in short supply in my life, Rennie, and I'm not waiting the rest of my days for it to magically appear. I make my own way in this world, and I'll form my own family.''

"And love them?''

"Any children, certainly."

"And your wife?''

"After time I'm sure I'll grow fond of her.''

"That is the coldest thing I've ever heard. Goodbye, Marc. Good luck with your business marriage.''

She stormed to the door and flung it wide, standing beside it, refusing to look at him.

When he reached the opening, he tilted her face again, to meet his eyes.

"I'll send Stuart over tomorrow to check out the books and help you set up your accounts. Did you call your suppliers about a quantity discount?''

"I said I would, didn't I?''

"Just checking. I don't leave much to chance, too many screwups happen if I don't follow up.''

"I'm not your responsibility," she said, her teeth clamped tightly together.

"Just protecting my investment," he said smoothly. Dropping a light kiss against her mouth, he walked down the hallway, wincing when he heard her door slam shut behind him. He wondered idly if the neighbors were used to it, or was this a first. He bet she never slammed the door behind Joseph Thurmond Sanger the Fourth.

But at least he knew tonight she had not been with her friend Joe. It eased the burning in his chest a little.

"Got a minute?" Stuart stood in the door to Marc's office the next afternoon.

"Sure, come in. What's up?" Marc leaned back in his chair and motioned his chief accountant to a chair.

"About Rennie Morgan's business. You asked me to send someone over there to set her up with proper accounts. I sent Nancy Brewer. She got back a little while ago. Apparently your friend Ms. Morgan has decided she doesn't need our help."

"What?"

"She politely but very firmly told Nancy to take a hike." Stuart shrugged. "Nancy did as she was told and left."

"Any reasons given?" Marc asked.

"Just that she had been managing her business since she started and she didn't need any help now, thank you very much."

"She's going to run it into the ground the way she's going. And she most definitely needs some help to get the mess straightened out. It's my investment I'm protecting," Marc said.

"Let me know if you want me to send Nancy out again."

"Right." Marc waited until Stuart left before reaching for the phone. Rennie's attitude was beginning to annoy him.

Eve answered. Déjà vu, Marc thought. "I want to speak to Rennie."

"She's not here." Gone was the helpful attitude that had marked her earlier reception.

"When do you expect her?"

"Not until tomorrow. I'll tell her you called, if you like," Eve said.

"Is she home?"

"Not that I know of. She had business to take care of. That's all she said, so you can ask a dozen questions, but I truly don't know."

"Tell her to call me when you hear from her, would you?"

Marc hung up after obtaining Eve's assurance she'd let Rennie know he'd called. He dialed her home, got an answering machine. Was that new? When he tried the other day, the phone had just rung and rung. Where was she? And what game was she playing now? He'd told her he planned to send an accountant. She didn't argue with him about it. Why the refusal to allow Nancy to set up her books?

Glancing at his calendar, he noted there was nothing after his two o'clock appointment. He'd take a quick drive to Union Street and see if Rennie had returned. If she hadn't, maybe he could get some information from Eve.

When he walked into the boutique three hours later, Marc felt the same as he'd experienced once before—like a stranger in an alien place. The ruffles and lace setting remained foreign to him, made to suit the fancy of women at their most feminine. He studied the lovely dress on the mannequin while he waited for someone to realize he was there. Even a man could realize how fancy it was and how it could represent the fantasy every woman wanted for a wedding day. For a moment he wondered about his own parents' wedding. Had his mother worn such a dress? Had she and his father been full of dreams and plans for a wonderful future? Or had it been a hurried-up affair, hastily planned and hastily executed? He'd never know. There was no one left to tell him.

He never saw a wedding picture, nor signs of a fancy dress like this. And he'd been so young when she left. His father had never spoken kindly about his wife once gone.

The dress looked small. He bet it would fit Rennie like a glove. Had she tried it on when it first arrived? Or maybe after the client had canceled the order? He could envision her wearing it. The lace would be beautiful against her skin, the soft white tone virginal and ethereal. Would she wear her hair in the froth of curls or slick it back into some elaborate style to suit a special occasion? He knew she'd be barefoot beneath the long skirt. Even on her wedding day. He'd be willing to make a large bet on that.

"Hello, Mr. Foster. Rennie still hasn't returned. I really don't expect her today."

Eve came from the back, stood behind the counter as if putting a barrier between them. For a moment Marc wondered if she felt safer or more in control with the solid wood and glass to hide behind.

"I sent an accountant over this morning to see about setting up the business's accounts," he said.

"Rennie doesn't need help there, she said," Eve replied. "And I do believe it is still her business. She gets to make the decisions."

"It won't be her business for long if she runs it into the ground because of sloppy accounting practices." Frustrated, Marc glared at the woman.

"I wouldn't know about that. Rennie handles her own business affairs. Was there something else?" A hint of antagonism colored her voice.

"I tried her home, she's not there."

Eve remained silent, her eyes gravely studying him.

"Do you know where she is?"

She shook her head. "No."

"Why did she take off after sending Nancy away?"

"She only said she had to see a man about a loan. I thought she was going to see you until you called."

See a man about a loan? Had she come to the office after he left? Was she looking for him even as he stood here searching for her?

"Can I use the phone?"

"Sure." She indicated the white wall phone near the door to the back room. "That's an extension for customers. Help yourself." She reached into the glass cabinet to needlessly straighten some lacy garters while Marc punched in his office number.

"Rachel, did Rennie Morgan stop by this afternoon?"

"No. Was she expected? I didn't have her noted on the calendar."

"I wasn't expecting her, just thought she might have stopped by. Or called?"

"No."

"I'll be back within the hour."

"We'll be here."

Marc saw the special delivery envelope as soon as he entered his office.

"I put that on your desk. The messenger said it was urgent," Rachel said, following him to the door of his office. "It was marked personal, so I didn't open it."

"Thanks, Rachel."

She smiled and nodded, pulling the door closed to give him privacy.

Shrugging out of his suit jacket, Marc tossed it across a chair. He picked up the envelope, mentally reviewing all the deals that were cooking. Nothing of such immediacy came to mind. He slit the envelope and drew out a letter, and a check.

Dear Marc:
Enclosed is a check in the full amount that Brides and Bows owes your firm. I consider our business association ended. Best of luck in finding your perfect wife.

Sincerely,
Rennie Morgan

He glanced at the cashier's check. He'd have to get Stuart to run a balance, but it looked as if it was made out for the full amount.

"Hell's bells, Rennie, what do you think you're doing?" he murmured as he stared at the letter again. Where had she gotten the money? It was a hefty sum, not easily raised. Certainly no bank would have advanced her the money—not based on her track record and the deplorable state of her books.

And why? He walked to the window and gazed out over the high-rise buildings of San Francisco. Why had she so abruptly severed their relationship? Had he come on too strongly last night?

Damn, she'd kissed him back.

Then cried.

He thought they were developing a friendship. He'd never had one with a woman before, and it proved to be a novel experience. Had he misread the signs? He didn't think so. Dammit, she had some explaining to do. Sending a letter and a check wasn't the way to end a friendship. She should have at least had the decency to confront him in person. He'd fix that.

He spun around and crossed to his desk, reaching for the phone.

By nine-thirty that night, Marc was about to give up. He'd called Rennie's home all afternoon and evening. The answering machine responded faithfully each time. Was she there screening her calls? He didn't think it likely. She was too up front and honest to hide behind a mechanical device. And he'd tried to tone down his anger. At least after the first five or six messages.

Where was she?

He reached for his phone file and looked up Keith's number. In seconds he had his friend on the phone.

"Hi, Marc, what's up?"

"Do you know where Rennie is?"

"Was it my turn to watch her?" Keith asked jovially.

"This is serious. Do you know where she is?" Marc was in no mood for jokes from Keith. He wanted to find Rennie.

"No. What's wrong? I would guess she's home."

"She's not answering her phone. And she's not at Brides and Bows. I need to find her."

"What's going on with the two of you? I thought Rennie was helping you filter out your perfect wife," Keith said. "Then at Toddy's party, you show up as Rennie's date. That's after coming to Mom's house that Sunday for the barbecue. And after I heard about you and Rennie having lunch at the London Pub."

"She's doing just what you said, introducing me to prospective candidates. But we've run into a snag and I need to get in touch with her."

"If she isn't home, she's probably out on a date. Catch her tomorrow."

"Tonight," Marc insisted.

Keith didn't speak for a long moment. "If you are pulling one of your business deals where my cousin gets the short end—"

"I'm not pulling anything. We had an agreement—never mind. I just want to talk to Rennie, as soon as possible."

"She could be on a date."

"I don't think so. She left work early and hasn't been home, as far as I can tell."

"You've been trying to reach her?"

"All afternoon. She's got an answering machine."

"Since when? Rennie said she didn't like them. She liked people to call her back if she doesn't answer. And if she's home, she likes phone calls, you know she likes to talk."

"I wouldn't have guessed," Marc said dryly.

Keith chuckled. "She does run on a bit sometimes. But she's a wonderful person."

"I agree. See if you can find out where she is, will you, Keith?"

"Right. I'll call you back when I find out something."

"I'm at the office. I'm leaving in a few minutes."

"Sounds like Rennie had the right of it, lecturing you on your workaholic tendencies."

"Yeah, maybe so. Call me when you find out where she is."

Marc drove from the office to Rennie's apartment. The windows were dark. He didn't bother to go up. While he could see her refusing to answer the phone, letting the answering machine respond to make sure she didn't answer his call, he couldn't picture her sitting alone in the dark all night. She was not home.

Reaching his condo, Marc checked his answering machine. No blinking light. Keith hadn't called yet. He tossed his suit coat on the back of the sofa and headed for the kitchen. A sandwich would tide him over. How long before Keith called?

At midnight Marc called Keith.

"Keith, what did you find out?"

"Marc? Nothing, I said I'd call you when I had something. I checked with a few friends, no one has seen her. But it was already late when you called. It would be worth my life to call Aunt Susan or my mom so late unless it was a damned emergency. I'll check with them in the morning. I said I'd call you when I heard something. Hey, man, what's up? I've never seen you push so hard for something like this."

"Just tying up some loose ends," Marc hedged. No sense telling Keith the entire story, at least until he himself figured out what it was.

He hung up the phone. On the table was the paper on which he'd scribbled Ellen's phone number. He picked it up and crushed it into a ball. Why would he want to date Ellen Naylor when he could spend time with Rennie? In fact, who was he kidding that he wanted some sleek sophisticated woman to be his wife?

He wanted Rennie.

It was time to forget his elaborate, sterile plan to find a paragon of a wife like some men bought racehorses. Before Rennie, he thought the plan a sound one. Now he wanted more.

He wanted a warm, loving woman to come home to. Wanted to finish work early so he could share dinner, and the tasks leading up to the meal. Wanted to spend evenings together, talking about their days, planning for a long future. He wanted Rennie in that future, to fascinate him with her chatter, to bring a balance to his own narrow focus on life. Her rosy view of life differed drastically, maybe he could balance her views. Together they could be stronger than each was alone.

He loved Rennie Morgan!

Marc pitched the balled paper into a trash can and headed for the kitchen. He needed a drink, a strong one. And then he'd look at the obvious. How long had he been in love with her? After a lifetime of denying there was such an emotion as love, of being convinced that it didn't exist, he'd fallen under its spell almost without being aware of it.

He couldn't imagine a future with another woman. He wanted Rennie.

One thing he prided himself on was the ability to move with the flow, when deals turned, he was quick to react, quick to formulate new strategy and move in a new direction. He could do the same with his life.

First he'd find Rennie. Then tell her he loved her. Surely she loved him in return.

He reached for a glass and the whiskey bottle. Taking a sip of the amber liquid, he contemplated the possibility that she did not. She'd not been anxious to help him find a possible life mate, yet that had not been from any selfish self-interest, but merely her belief that his stated goal was a poor reason to marry. Turned out she was right. She'd spent time with him, but always with the end goal of finding him a bride, another woman for his bride.

She didn't approve of many facets of his life, from his long working hours to his cold way of analyzing a relationship and moving toward his goal. He wasn't perfect. The more he thought about it, the less he found to make him suspect she did love him. She'd certainly pointed out how crazy she thought his goal of finding the perfect wife was.

Rennie would not be perfect, either. She'd probably drive him crazy a dozen times a year. But she would also perfect his world, bringing sunshine and laughter where there had only been work and more work and long dreary nights.

They had started building a friendship, spent many hours together companionably. He could be patient, wait for her to fall in love with him. Do things she liked. He was good at strategizing. He could figure out what she wanted and make sure she got it. Somehow along the way he had to make sure she knew he no longer wanted another woman. That she'd been right, his way of acquiring a wife was wrong.

But would she fall in love with him? He wasn't Joseph Thurmond Sanger the Fourth. He didn't have a family name worth a hill of beans. He had some money, but she seemed singularly unimpressed with wealth.

That led to his wondering for the one hundredth time where she'd gotten the money today to pay off the loan from Foster Associates.

Pacing a path in the living room carpet, he sipped the drink, remembering all the hours he'd spent with Rennie. How could he not have suspected where they were heading? He'd dated plenty of women before, casually, with no ties, no expectations. But he never dressed casually and went to their apartments just to listen to them talk about their job. Never went to family parties. Never spent a day wandering around San Francisco, eating at the tourist traps and riding the cable cars.

And never before felt so lost and found in the blue of a woman's eyes.

"Where the hell are you, Rennie?" he asked aloud.

Marc was still home the next morning when the phone rang. He'd dressed in jeans and a casual shirt. He did not plan to go into the office—not until he found Rennie and talked with her.

"You sorry bastard, what did you do to her?" Keith's accusing voice sounded in Marc's ear when he picked up the phone.

"I didn't do anything. What did she say I did?"

"Nothing to me, I told you I didn't know where she was. But I've found out quite a bit, and want to know what you did to chase her away."

Marc gripped the receiver tightly, but kept his voice cool. "I am rather curious about that myself. I saw her night before last, the next thing I knew, she sends me a check for the full amount of the investment Foster's made and told me she could no longer help find me a wife."

"What else?"

Marc could almost feel the heat of Keith's anger.

"Nothing else."

"Dammit, Marc, I'm not buying. Rennie's never before felt she had to leave town over something."

"Leave town?"

"And she borrowed some money from Theo. I can't imagine what she went through to do that. She always swore she wouldn't take his money, even though he offered to help her out many times. He's crazy about her and wants to do things for her like he does her mother."

"Theo, of course. I wondered where she got the money."

"Have you heard anything I've said? I want some answers, and I want them now!"

"Hold on, Keith. I told you, I don't know what is going on, that's why I want to talk with Rennie. Where is she?"

Keith hesitated.

"Come on, Keith. I'm not going to hurt her. I just want to talk to her."

"Why should I trust anything you say? You are apparently the reason she left. Why tell you where she's gone? Leave her alone, Marc."

Marc closed his eyes. "Keith, I can't."

"Sure you can. Leave my cousin the hell alone! Find your own damn trophy wife, you have enough background about the eligible women. It was a dumb idea, I can't believe I even suggested it."

"I thought at first you were setting me up with your cousin," Marc said slowly, opening his eyes. He remembered seeing Rennie for the first time. Involuntarily he smiled.

"That would be like oil and water."

"Opposites attract."

"Right, you're saying you are attracted to Rennie?" Keith scoffed.

Marc didn't respond.

"Marc? You aren't saying you are attracted to Rennie?" Incredulity replaced the sarcasm.

"Yes, I am saying it. In fact I'll go one step farther than that, but only to Rennie."

"God, I don't believe this. You and Rennie? No wonder she ran."

"Where is she, Keith?"

If he didn't tell him, Marc had no qualms about driving over to his place and finding a way to make him tell.

"Lake Tahoe. The family has a huge home in Stateline. She went there to think things through. That's what she told her mother. I can't believe you fell for Rennie. She's not anything like Suzanne Barclay."

"I know. Except for the party last Saturday when she

dressed to the nines, she has never fit my image of what I wanted. But it was just an image. She's real. And I want her.''

Keith laughed. ''Good luck, pal. You're going to need it. I can't see Rennie giving in easily. Especially after whatever happened to drive her away.''

''I don't know what drove her away. That's why I'm trying to find her, to discover what went wrong.''

What went wrong beyond the obvious, having the woman he wanted assigned the task of locating a wife for him. He'd been a fool.

Keith gave him directions to the house at Lake Tahoe, and told Marc to call him when he returned to the city. He wanted to know the outcome.

Taking time to pack a small bag, and make two stops, Marc then headed for Lake Tahoe. He'd find Rennie, and get her to explain why she'd paid off the debt and why she'd left the city so precipitously.

And then maybe he'd figure out a way to introduce the idea of the two of them seeing each other. Dating. With the end view the possibility of marriage.

He hoped she'd at least listen to him. He wasn't sure what he'd do if she didn't.

It was late by the time he reached Stateline. The motels and chalets, the shops and businesses that lined the road on the California side were busy. The high-rise buildings that comprised the casinos and hotels on the Nevada side reflected the setting sun in the myriad windows. He drove through the busy street, wondering if it was ever quiet in this town. Two miles beyond the strip he found the road Keith had named. Turning, he followed it down to the lake, then along the water's edge until he found the house. There was a small car parked in the driveway.

He realized he didn't know what kind of car she drove. There were a million other facts about her he didn't know yet. But discovering everything about her would prove fascinating, of that he was sure. If she'd let him.

There was still that.

CHAPTER TEN

RENNIE opened the door to his knock. Upon recognizing him, she tried to slam it shut. Marc stuck his foot in the opening, insuring she couldn't lock him out.

"I want to talk to you," he said, his hand gripping the edge of the door, pushing against it until she gave up and stepped back.

"I would think you would get a hint that I don't want to talk to you! Who told you I was here? Keith, I bet. How did he find out? I might have known my male cousin would bond with his male friend and throw his female relative to the wolves."

"Wolves?" Marc raised an eyebrow. The relief at finding her dimmed a bit at the obvious lack of welcome in her eyes. In fact, he looked closer, she looked as if she'd been crying again. "So am I cast as the big bad wolf?"

She shrugged. "If the shoe fits," she said, turning away, giving up on an attempt to shut him out.

Marc took advantage and stepped inside, closing the door behind him. He followed her into the spacious living room. For a moment the breathtaking view from the huge picture window drew his attention. The snow-covered mountains that rimmed Lake Tahoe were silhouetted in the dying rays of the sun, the lake dark and mysterious in the evening shadows. But the grandeur of the scene couldn't be hidden by the darkness. It was spectacular. He'd like to see the view in all seasons and all times of the day.

"Nice view," he commented, shifting his gaze to Rennie. Beautiful as it was, it didn't compare with the woman before him.

"Came with the house," she said flippantly. "What are you doing here?" She glared at him.

"I came to talk to you."

"I don't have anything to say. I sent you a check for the full amount I owed your company. Our association is ended."

"Wasn't there more between us than business, Rennie?" he asked. If she didn't feel anything for him, his task would be all the harder. But he was used to overcoming tremendous odds to succeed. He'd done it in business, he'd do it with his personal life. He wanted her at his side the rest of his life. He'd do whatever it took to achieve that end.

She looked at him warily, suspicion forming in her face. "Like what?"

He wanted her to smile, to see the dancing light in her eyes, to have her exuberance back in full force. What had gone wrong? And how could he get them back on track? Especially if she wasn't interested. Now that the time was at hand, he became unsure. Unused to expressing his feelings, except anger, which he handled better each year, he was at a loss. If she didn't care something for him, he would be a total idiot to hand her the weapon of his true feelings. Yet someone had to make a move.

"How did you get the money to repay the loan?"

"That's not your affair," she said, watching him warily.

"Satisfy my curiosity."

"I asked Theo, he said yes."

He nodded and took a step closer. "Thought you

didn't want to take advantage of Theo's generosity and ask him for the start-up money.''

"I didn't.''

"But?''

"But he's always offered and I saw it as a way to end this farce between us.'' She turned and gazed out the window.

Marc wondered if she saw the beauty of the scenery, or was too caught up in the conversation to notice.

"I thought we had a good working relationship.''

"Shows how much you know,'' she muttered.

He stepped closer. He could smell the fragrance of her hair, the sweet scent that was Rennie.

"I like you, Rennie. I like spending time with you.''

"You spent time with me as a way to find your ideal wife,'' she said flatly.

"Not just for that. What about Saturday when we wandered around the city together?''

"I thought you were trying to one-up Joe.''

He frowned. That had been part of the reason he'd asked her out. Primarily he wanted to make sure she knew she could enjoy being with him more than being with Joe. He hated thinking about her with the doctor. The two of them had so much in common with mutual backgrounds and friends. How could an outsider hope to compete? But the day spent together had been fun. And the evenings. And the trip to her aunt's. Playing horse-shoes. Everything he'd done with her had been fun. It was Rennie's special gift, making the most mundane task an exciting adventure.

"I wanted to spend the day with you. It had nothing to do with Joseph Thurmond Sanger,'' he lied.

"I can't imagine why.''

"You can't be that dense. You are delightful to be

around. Funny, witty. You fairly sparkle with an enthusiasm that is totally refreshing. And that emotion is missing from most of the people I know these days. Everyone else is deadly serious about things.''

"Like you. Cutthroat business is the be all and end all, right?'' She moved nervously, flicking a quick glance his way, then looking back out the window.

"Not always.'' Used to reading people, Marc realized he didn't have that knack with Rennie. She threw him completely.

"Give me a break, Marc. You employed those ends to finding a wife. You made a list of requirements, set a goal and then relentlessly pursued it.''

"Not anymore.''

"What does that mean? Did you call Ellen? Have you already made plans for a wedding?'' She turned around, stark horror displayed on her face. She took a breath and looked at the ashes in the fireplace.

He laughed softly. Had that look meant something? He grabbed hold to the thought.

"Even the fastest worker in the world would find it a bit hard to meet a woman last Saturday night and arrange a marriage by now. I haven't called her. Probably won't ever have an occasion to call her.''

"I thought she met your requirements.''

"I've rethought those requirements, modified them a bit.''

"Oh?'' She glanced at him in surprise. She motioned to the sofa. "Do you want to sit down or something? Since you seem to be staying. I want you to leave, but I don't suppose my desires will be met in this. You are bigger than I am, I can't force you out, so the only choice left is to hear what you have to say and then maybe you'll leave.''

"Desires are something else we can talk about. But maybe we should clear the air on the wife issue first."

"Definitely." She sat primly on the edge of a chair near the massive stone fireplace. Marc considered letting her remain there, but decided against it. He'd go for broke in this confrontation. He had his goal firmly in mind and he would use all his negotiating skills to bring about the desired end. But in the meantime, skills or not, he wanted her close. He wanted to hold her. Touch her. Connect with her.

Reaching for her hand, he pulled her up. Ignoring her exclamation, he stepped across to the sofa and sat down, pulling her beside him, firmly holding her hand, his fingers threading through hers.

"Let me go!" She struggled briefly to escape. He tightened his grip.

"Not yet. I want to talk to you. And I'm not taking any chances that you'll dash away again. Sit still until I'm finished. If you still want to move after that, I'll let you go."

She glared at him. "If I want to move? I want you to leave and I don't plan to follow!"

Marc smiled. At least the indifference was gone. Fire lit her eyes, her cheeks glowed with color.

"I'm not sure where to start," he said after a moment. He wasn't sure he wanted to say anything. What he wanted to do was pull her onto his lap and kiss her until dawn. More than kiss her, make love with her. Share his hopes and dreams, learn more of hers. Bind her to him so tightly she would never wish to leave.

"Great, you track me down when I'm trying to avoid seeing you, insist you have to talk to me, then can't decide where to start. Just say what you think you have to say and leave!"

"Your note and check surprised me," he began.

"I didn't want to be involved anymore," she said stiffly. "Find your own wife."

"It must have been hard to ask your stepfather for a loan when you had resisted so long."

She stared straight ahead, her profile all he could see. But he felt the stiffening in her body.

"Rennie, you didn't have to do that."

"I wanted out of our deal. With no loan to Foster Associates, I'd be free."

"You could have said something. At least brought me the check, rather than send it by messenger."

She looked at him then, anger flashing in her blue eyes. "In case it escaped your notice, I was trying to avoid you. Why do you think I came to Lake Tahoe? I knew you'd be on the phone or at my apartment to demand your pound of flesh. I was trying to avoid you. Wait until I get my hands on Keith. I'll wring his neck. Family should count more than the old boy network. Get him to help you find a bride!"

"I know who I want to marry. And I know all about her background, not that it's important anymore. The question isn't who I want, but if she'll have me," he said slowly. He looked at their linked hands, suddenly more nervous than he'd ever been, even when closing his first million-dollar deal.

Rennie tossed her head, turning away and prying at his fingers. He held firm.

"I'm glad for you. If you have your wife lined up, why are you here?"

"I said I know who I want to marry, who I want to live the rest of my life with. But I'm not sure she feels the same."

"Offer her enough money, or jewelry, or unlimited

entertaining. Isn't that what you want in a wife?" she said bitterly.

"I thought I did, but something changed along the way. And I didn't quite realize how much I've changed until yesterday."

"Yesterday?" She looked at him. The curiosity in her gaze was heartening. He had her attention now. If he could glean some of her feelings before exposing all of his, he'd feel better about the outcome.

"When I got your letter and then couldn't reach you."

"What does that have to do with anything?"

"I went by the shop, you know. Eve said you were gone, but I wasn't sure if she was telling the truth or not."

"She was, I left as soon as I sent the check. I knew you'd be upset."

"Upset?" he asked mildly. She didn't have a clue to how he'd felt.

"So you went to the shop. I hope you didn't intimidate Eve."

"Like I do you?"

She shrugged. "I don't intimidate very easily."

"I have never intimidated you a minute in your life," he commented. "A rather interesting turn of events, when I think about it. You are probably the only person I can say that about."

"Let's not analyze everything to death. That's the businessman in you, I suppose. Or is it just a male thing? Things are the way they are," she snapped.

"I know, let's look at it through rosy glasses, seeing only the wonderful aspects of everything and ignoring anything that doesn't fit our picture of how things should be."

The glimmer of a smile touched her. "I don't ignore everything that doesn't fit my picture," she defended.

"While I waited for Eve to come out from the back room, I studied that pretty wedding dress on the mannequin. The one you got stuck with. You'd look lovely in it. Have you ever tried it on?"

"The wedding dress? Sure. When the client canceled her order, I was so mad. Then I looked at the dress and couldn't resist trying it on. It's in my size, you know."

"And I bet you looked like a dream. Would you wear your hair in some elaborate style, or like you normally do?"

"Oh, right, I'm going to wear an elegant wedding gown with this mop of curls? I'd have it styled, romantic and old-fashioned. If I ever had an occasion to wear it for real, I mean. Which I don't. I can't believe you even glanced at the dress, much less imagined me in it."

"I imagine you in a lot of things." And out of them, too, but he thought it prudent to refrain from mentioning that at this juncture.

"Like what?" She was intrigued, he could see it. Now if he just didn't come on too fast. He wanted her to relax, consider what he planned to propose.

"I see us taking walks around the city during the nice weather, maybe riding the cable cars again. I see you at Christmas delightfully choosing presents for family and friends, excited about decorating a tree and following all the traditions of the holiday. I see you cooking dinner, reading a book curled up in a chair, with your feet bare." He glanced down. Socks covered her toes, but there were no shoes in evidence.

"For you, Marc, that's almost poetic. What's the catch?" she asked warily.

"No catch. I like thinking about you."

"In between thinking of who you'd like to marry, which socialite would be best suited for the honor of Mrs. Marc Foster?"

He sighed. He knew this wouldn't be easy. "Sometimes when a goal is made, all the facts aren't known. Reassessing the situation leads to change."

"Meaning?"

"Meaning, could we forget about looking for a paragon for a wife?"

She looked at him, her eyes wide and questioning.

"I like spending time with you," he continued. The emotions in his chest threatened to burst through. Why didn't she say something? Was he making a hash of this? He took a breath, it was do or die time. "Rennie, I want you to marry me."

Her gaze never wavered. She stared at him as if he'd lost his mind. Slowly tears welled up in her eyes.

Oh, God, she was going to cry. He hadn't meant to make her cry!

"Rennie, don't cry. If you don't want to, that's okay. No, it's not okay, but I can live with it. Maybe the idea will grow on you. Don't cry."

She blinked and one tear spilled down her cheek. "You want to marry me?" she asked.

"Yes." His thumb brushed away the errant tear. Her skin was as silky as ever. He could hardly contain his urge to taste that soft skin, to kiss her and hold her and never let her go.

"Why?"

"Why? Why does a man normally want to marry a woman? So she'll be his wife."

"Oh, Marc!" She raised her eyes to the ceiling as if seeking inspiration. Looking back at him, she slowly shook her head.

Panic touched him. She was refusing? She couldn't. He wanted her like he'd never wanted anything else. More than the money that enabled him to turn his back on the kind of life he'd known as a child. More than some kind of entry into society. He would settle for life with Rennie any day. What he wasn't sure of was if he'd be able to live with her rejection.

"Don't say no just yet, listen to what I have to offer."

"Marc, I don't want to be a trophy bride. I told you my feelings in this matter at the very beginning. They haven't changed just because you think I might be suitable."

"But you haven't heard all I have to—"

"You have tons of material things and more money than should be legal. But that's not enough," she said gently, tears still shimmering in her eyes.

"You are right. It's not enough. I want you to share my life, Rennie, not my money. To be home when I get home, and nag me if I work late. Share tasks around the house, plan vacations together. Did you know I haven't had a real vacation in over ten years? I expect living with you would change that."

"Marc, I want more."

"You want commitment and loyalty and faithfulness and—" His voice closed up. Staring at her for some idea of how she felt, he could only feel a deepening sense of panic. She was not going to marry him. She would be kind when she said no, but he had nothing she wanted. He only had himself to offer. And that was nothing to compare with Joseph Thurmond Sanger the Fourth.

"And love, Marc. I want love."

He took a breath. "I can offer that, as well."

"What?"

He cleared his throat. "I love you, Rennie. I'm not quite sure how it happened, but it's true. I love you!"

Tears flooded again, but her smile grew huge. Confused, he tried to figure out what was happening. "Are you crying, or smiling?"

"Both." She pulled her hand free and flung herself into his arms, her own encircling his neck tightly. When she rested her face against his, he felt the dampness of her tears.

"Don't cry," he repeated.

"I'm so happy, I can't help it. I love you, Marc Foster. I've had a crush on you for years, and was thrilled when I first got to meet you. But you never even saw me. You wanted sleek and sophisticated, and that I'll never be."

"I don't know, you looked pretty sophisticated at the party last Saturday night."

"Oh, sure, once in a while I can do it, but it's not the real me, the twenty-four-hours-a-day me."

"No, it's not, and I wouldn't change a single thing about you. Say yes, Rennie. Marry me."

She pulled back a bit to look deep into his eyes. "I love you. Of course I'll marry you."

"Just needed to be sure. One of the first rules of business is never to assume."

She laughed and brushed the tears from her cheeks. "God, what an adventure. Me tied up with a died-in-the-wool businessman. Next thing I'll know Brides and Bows will be franchised and have boutiques across the country."

"If that is what you want—"

"No, silly, I'm just joking. I like my own little shop. It suits me. I'll want to keep working after we get married."

"Ultimatums already?" he asked lazily. The relief

flooded every inch of him. She was going to marry him. She loved him. He almost couldn't believe it. But she'd said yes and he'd hold her to it, no matter what. Hell, they were right in Nevada, they could be married tomorrow. That would link them forever.

"Not really. Do you mind that I work?"

"No." Right now he'd grant her anything. *She had said yes!*

"And when the kids come, I'll be able to take them to work. Of course I can cut back by then. Hire another assistant. Eve could be the manager."

"Already thinking ahead. Maybe you're more of a businesswoman than you think," he said. "How many kids are we planning?"

"Lots, don't you think? We were both only children, I missed having brothers and sisters. Of course Keith and Gloria came close."

"Speaking of Keith, maybe you could reconsider wringing his neck?"

She laughed and hugged him hard. "I love you, Marc. I hated thinking about you courting someone like Marcella when I wanted you to court me. But I sure don't fit all the criteria you listed. And I thought you didn't believe in love."

"I thought so, too. There hasn't been a lot of it in my life, Rennie. But when I got your letter, and then couldn't reach you, it brought home exactly what my life would be like if I didn't see you again. I knew it was love when I hated the thought of your having to go to Theo when you had fought against it for so long. I could practically feel the blow to your pride. I wish you had talked to me instead of throwing that note in my face."

"I didn't think I could. I was really hurting that you

seemed to be interested in Ellen and couldn't see me for the furniture. Somehow, after that first lunch, I thought you and I were a team. Then when you arranged to get Ellen's number without me, the reality of the situation hit me. You could ask her out and never see me again. I just couldn't stand it. I had to get away. And make sure there was nothing to tie us together. I didn't want to have to pretend to be happy at your marriage to another woman.''

"Ah, so that explains your attitude at the party. I couldn't figure that out.''

"I tried to hide it.''

"You succeeded. Maybe in fifty years or so, I'll be able to figure you out without your telling me.''

"Maybe. But then, where's the excitement and mystery?''

"I expect I'll always find it with you.''

When he kissed her, Marc felt as if he'd come home. The flighty, tousled, casual woman he loved bore little resemblance to the ideal woman he thought he wanted. Instead, Rennie brought sunshine and warmth into his life, and he wouldn't trade that for anything.

"It's time,'' Keith said.

Marc looked at him and nodded. He checked the tux one more time in the mirror. "I'm as ready as I'll ever be,'' he said grimly, wishing she had agreed to the quick wedding he'd wanted in Nevada.

Keith chuckled. "Thought you wanted to marry her.''

"I do. It's this wedding I'm not so sure about.''

"Hey, Brides and Bows planned it from beginning to end. It should go like clockwork.''

"I don't know why she couldn't have settled for a quick visit to a judge,'' Marc grumbled. But he should have known from the first that his romantic bride would settle for nothing less than the fairy-tale wedding of her dreams. At least the waiting was over. The months since he'd proposed had seemed endless. Only this last week when they began moving Rennie's things into his place had the reality of their marriage finally solidified. He'd been worried something would come up to cause a rift. No matter how often she told him she loved him, no matter how often he saw the love in her eyes, he still had trouble convincing himself it was real and lasting.

"Wait until you see her in her wedding dress, it'll be worth it," Keith said.

"I know." For a moment Marc turned to his friend. Keith had been cheated of his own wedding by Betsy's death. Only now, so many years later, could he relate to the pain and devastation his friend must have gone through, must still feel. He didn't know how he'd live through the days if something happened to Rennie.

"I appreciate your standing up with me," Marc said, reaching out to grip Keith's shoulder. This man had been his friend all his adult life. For the first time Marc truly appreciated the bond.

Keith smiled. "What's a friend for if not best man? Ready?"

"Yes."

Standing before the congregation at the huge church that had been Rennie's place of worship since childhood, Marc watched as the rainbow of bridesmaids walked down the aisle in tempo with the wedding music. Slowly he smiled. Rennie had picked an interesting group, Marcella, Julie, Suzanne, and Ellen. Keith's sister was maid of honor.

When the wedding party moved into place, the organ music changed and Marc looked at the back of the church. Rennie appeared, holding Theo's arm. Slowly they walked down the aisle.

His heart caught, began beating double time. She was so radiantly beautiful. And looked as sleek and sophisticated as he could ever have wanted. The dress that had once stood on a mannequin fit her like a dream. The veil that covered to her fingertips didn't hide the shining light of her smile, the sparkle in her blue eyes. He couldn't look anywhere but at the darling woman who would soon be his wife.

Theo handed her to Marc, made the proper response and moved to sit in the first pew beside Rennie's mother. Marc noticed this peripherally. He was too startled when he realized that she was shorter than normal—barefoot again. Sophisticated on the outside, his Rennie on the inside. He wouldn't have her any different.

Linking his hand with hers, linking his heart, they turned to face the minister who would link their lives forever.

Harlequin Romance®

Get ready to meet the world's most eligible bachelors: they're sexy, successful and, best of all, they're all yours!

Look out for these next two books:

September 1998:
WANTED: A PERFECT WIFE (#3521)
by Barbara McMahon

November 1998:
MY GIRL (#3529)
by Lucy Gordon

There are two sides to every relationship—and now it's his turn!

Available wherever Harlequin books are sold.

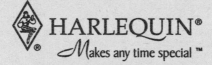

HARLEQUIN®
Makes any time special ™

Look us up on-line at: http://www.romance.net

HRBT3

Take 2 bestselling love stories FREE

Plus get a FREE surprise gift!

Special Limited-Time Offer

Mail to Harlequin Reader Service®

3010 Walden Avenue
P.O. Box 1867
Buffalo, N.Y. 14240-1867

YES! Please send me 2 free Harlequin Romance® novels and my free surprise gift. Then send me 6 brand-new novels every month, which I will receive months before they appear in bookstores. Bill me at the low price of $2.90 each plus 25¢ delivery and applicable sales tax if any*. That's the complete price, and a saving of over 10% off the cover prices—quite a bargain! I understand that accepting the books and gift places me under no obligation ever to buy any books. I can always return a shipment and cancel at any time. Even if I never buy another book from Harlequin, the 2 free books and the surprise gift are mine to keep forever.

116 HEN CH68

Name		
	(PLEASE PRINT)	
Address		Apt. No.
City	State	Zip

This offer is limited to one order per household and not valid to present Harlequin Romance® subscribers. *Terms and prices are subject to change without notice. Sales tax applicable in N.Y.

UROM-98

©1990 Harlequin Enterprises Limited

*The only way to be a bodyguard
is to stay as close as a lover...*

STAND BY ME

The relationship between bodyguard and client is always
close...sometimes too close for comfort. This September,
join in the adventure as three bodyguards, protecting three
very distracting and desirable charges, struggle not to cross
the line between business and pleasure.

STRONG ARMS OF THE LAW
by Dallas SCHULZE

NOT WITHOUT LOVE
by Roberta LEIGH

SOMETIMES A LADY
by Linda Randall WISDOM

*Sometimes danger makes
a strange bedfellow!*

Available September 1998 wherever
Harlequin and Silhouette books are sold.

HARLEQUIN® ▼ *Silhouette*®

Look us up on-line at: http://www.romance.net   PHBR998

Remember the magic of the film
It's a Wonderful Life?
The warmth and tender emotion of
Truly, Madly, Deeply?
The feel-good humor of *Heaven Can Wait*?

Well, even if we can't promise you angels that look like
Alan Rickman or Warren Beatty, starting in June in
Harlequin Romance®, we can promise a brand-new
miniseries: GUARDIAN ANGELS. Featuring all of your
favorite ingredients for a perfect novel: great heroes,
feisty heroines and a breathtaking romance—all with a
celestial spin.

Look for Guardian Angels in:

June 1998: THE BOSS, THE BABY AND THE BRIDE (#3508)
by Day Leclaire

August 1998: HEAVENLY HUSBAND (#3516)
by Carolyn Greene

October 1998: A GROOM FOR GWEN (#3524)
by Jeanne Allan

December 1998: GABRIEL'S MISSION (#3532)
by Margaret Way

**Falling in love sometimes needs a little help
from above!**

Available wherever Harlequin books are sold.

Look us up on-line at: http://www.romance.net

HRGA

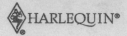

Not The Same Old Story!

 HARLEQUIN PRESENTS®
Exciting, glamorous romance stories that take readers around the world.

Harlequin Romance®
Sparkling, fresh and tender love stories that bring you pure romance.

HARLEQUIN® *Temptation*
Bold and adventurous—Temptation is strong women, bad boys, great sex!

HARLEQUIN SUPERROMANCE®
Provocative and realistic stories that celebrate life and love.

 HARLEQUIN® AMERICAN ROMANCE®
Contemporary fairy tales—where anything is possible and where dreams come true.

 HARLEQUIN® INTRIGUE®
Heart-stopping, suspenseful adventures that combine the best of romance and mystery.

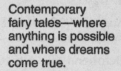 LOVE & LAUGHTER™
Humorous and romantic stories that capture the lighter side of love.

Look us up on-line at: http://www.romance.net   HGENERIC